He wanted another chance.

Whatever else he'd have to give up, whatever else was waiting for him at the end of his journey, Frank wanted Kate in his arms.

In his bed.

The knowing shot through him, burned hot as racing fuel in his chest, churned in his gut. He wanted her, and he didn't want to wait.

But if he pushed too hard, he'd risk losing her, the way he'd lost everything else. And more. He'd risk damaging the boy. It was best to keep his distance. From them both.

Life was just a series of choices, and he'd made so many wrong ones. This time he vowed to do things right....

Dear Reader,

Brides, babies and families...that's just what Special Edition has in store for you this August! All this and more from some of your favorite authors.

Our THAT'S MY BABY! title for this month is *Of Texas Ladies, Cowboys...and Babies,* by popular Silhouette Romance author Jodi O'Donnell. In her first book for Special Edition, Jodi tells of a still young and graceful grandmother-to-be who unexpectedly finds herself in the family way! Fans of Jodi's latest Romance novel, *Daddy Was a Cowboy,* won't want to miss this spin-off title!

This month, GREAT EXPECTATIONS, the wonderful new series of family and homecoming by Andrea Edwards, continues with *A Father's Gift.* And summer just wouldn't be right without a wedding, so we present *A Bride for John,* the second book of Trisha Alexander's newest series, THREE BRIDES AND A BABY. Beginning this month is a new miniseries from veteran author Pat Warren, REUNION. Three siblings must find each other as they search for true love. It all begins with one sister's story in *A Home for Hannah.*

Also joining the Special Edition family this month is reader favorite and Silhouette Romance author Stella Bagwell. Her first title for Special Edition is *Found: One Runaway Bride.* And returning to Special Edition this August is Carolyn Seabaugh with *Just a Family Man,* as the lives of one woman and her son are forever changed when an irresistible man walks into their café in the wild West.

This truly is a month packed with summer fun and romance! I hope you enjoy each and every story to come!

Sincerely,
Tara Gavin, Senior Editor

Please address questions and book requests to:
Silhouette Reader Service
U.S.: 3010 Walden Ave., P.O. Box 1325, Buffalo, NY 14269
Canadian: P.O. Box 609, Fort Erie, Ont. L2A 5X3

CAROLYN SEABAUGH

JUST A FAMILY MAN

SPECIAL EDITION®

Published by Silhouette Books

America's Publisher of Contemporary Romance

For Jack

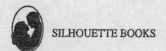

SILHOUETTE BOOKS

ISBN 0-373-24050-3

JUST A FAMILY MAN

Printed in U.S.A.

CAROLYN SEABAUGH

writes to revisit the many places she's lived, creating stories for the people who've called those places home. "The Colorado Rockies, the tall green hills of Oklahoma, the smell of oregano growing wild on the Texas plateaus, the wildflowers of Alaska's spring…a place gets in your soul and whispers its secrets if you let it," she says. Presently, Carolyn lives in Maryland with her husband, Jack, and their two beloved Labrador retrievers, Misty and Bear.

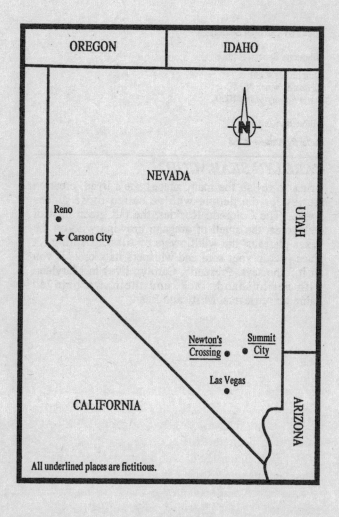

OREGON

IDAHO

NEVADA

Reno

★ Carson City

UTAH

Newton's
Crossing

Summit
City

Las Vegas

CALIFORNIA

ARIZONA

All underlined places are fictitious.

Chapter One

Out on the highway a silver semi screeched to a halt at the blinking stoplight, cut a wide right, then rolled toward the only café in Newton's Crossing, Nevada, population five and no longer counting.

Kate Prescott had just thrown the switch to the tall two-armed cactus sign out in front of the café. Lime-green neon pulsed into the gathering dusk. First the right arm lit, then the left, then the fat green body. Saguaro Café and Rooms came on, minus its final *s*.

"It's going the way of the No Vacancy sign," Kate said to no one in particular.

Not that it mattered. All six motel units hadn't rented at once since longer than she could remember.

Kate waved and two sharp blasts from an air horn responded, Trav's trademark. He pulled the big rig across the street, up to two ancient crimson-coated gas pumps that stood guard like sentinels over the deserted garage and a scattering of other low buildings.

A cloud of dust joined the sand stirred up by the semi and rolled like a tumbleweed toward the café. The passenger door opened. A man swung out of the truck's cab. A man dressed in black, a stranger. A tall man with a strong, proud back.

"Trav's got someone with him," Kate said across the small knot of customers.

The big cook smacked his spatula hard on the griddle.

At the counter a waitress spun around, dark eyes snapping and black braids flying. "Guess Bo thought you folks would be the only hungry ones in southeast Nevada this evening," she said.

"Aw, hush up, Mattie. I'm out of fries, that's all."

Kate turned from the window. "Bobby—"

"Sure, Mom, be back in a flash."

Kate caught the screen door as nine-and-a-half years of all-boy energy dashed out. Bobby would be up the rocky hill and back down with a bag of fries from the extra freezer at the house before Trav had finished filling his tank, she knew.

"That boy of yours can't sit still for a minute," Bobby's teacher said from the center table. "No wonder his math is slipping again."

Kate moved over to clear Ev White's table, now and then glancing out the window. The man was talking to Trav. Long legs, slim hips, broad shoulders. *Like a matador.* A warning followed the thought, hazy as a shimmering mirage.

"You saw his last test?"

"Hmm? Oh. Bobby always lapses a little in the spring. We were the same when we were kids, Ev. Remember?"

"You're *far* too easy on that boy, Kate Prescott, though it's no wonder." She lowered her voice. "Just take one look at the help around here."

Kate hoped they hadn't heard. Sure, Bo was a bit unkempt and lax about ordering supplies, and Mattie would rather fuss at her husband than set a table or wash a dish. But they were all she and Bobby had, and she was all they had, too. Evelyn White, on the other hand, had no one.

"A little more coffee, Ev? I've got a fresh pot brewing in the back. It's that Frisco blend you like so much."

"Why not? I'm none too eager to get home and grade papers."

Moments later, just as Kate left the dish room, the tall man came through the café's front door.

Each paused on opposite thresholds—she with a bag of frozen fries in one hand and a full coffeepot in the other, he with the last light of evening framing his shoulders in the doorway. A hard-handsome face, Kate thought, with olive skin that would darken in the hot Nevada sun as easily as her own turned pink and burned.

The man moved forward. Conversation stopped as everyone took in the leather dress boots, expensive black suit, gold watchband glinting at his cuff. Hair thick and rich and dark as a desert midnight curled down to his collar. *Gambler on his way to Vegas?*

No. He didn't have a gambler's shifting gaze. He looked directly at her, his eyes not dark as she'd expected but a startling silver blue, knife sharp despite obvious fatigue. She met them evenly.

"There's a table in the back corner," Kate said. The man nodded and turned toward the rear of the café, and the customers went back to their idle chatter.

"We off on another rescue mission?" Bo muttered as she passed him the fries.

"I don't think he needs rescuing. Maybe some rest."

"He's hitching, ain't he? Besides, I saw your look. Same one you wore when you took in me and Mattie. Saw his too. You better watch out, Kate."

"*You'd* better watch out, Bo Thompson. Don't burn these fries, they're the last of the lot."

The big cook grunted and flipped the dial on the fryer a notch lower.

Kate worked her way down the counter with the coffeepot, supplying cream to those she knew took it, checking the sugar dispensers at the same time. Soon she'd move over to the tables, the one near the door with an elderly couple, Ev's in the middle, the one toward the back with the stranger. In a moment Trav would join him. She'd fill both cups at once.

The café's door swung open again and Kate looked up, expecting the trucker. The man at the table looked up, too.

The state trooper's gaze swept the small café, lingered on the woman, then moved on to Frank's table.

"Hell of a night to be on the road," the trooper said, moving toward him. "Hate to see it hot so early. Damn cruiser overheats something fierce."

"Trade 'er in," the cook called out. "Us taxpayers want to keep you ridin' in style, *Officer* MacMillan."

A ripple of laughter slid through the café, diffusing when it reached Frank's table.

Should he smile? Put the uniformed man at his ease? A muscle jumped at the corner of Frank's mouth. He hooked a boot on the lower rung of the empty chair opposite and pulled it in. The trooper's eyes locked hard on his.

Then the woman was there, pouring his coffee.

"Mattie's got your place set over at the counter, Mac, and your steak's on the grill. Cherry pie's for dessert."

The trooper coughed and color rose around his prominent ears. "Thanks, Kate."

Someone at the counter chuckled. The trooper straddled a stool, glaring right and left.

Her tone had been slow and quiet, Frank thought, as loose as the soft brown braid that hung down her back, as smooth and warming as the coffee flowing into his cup. He watched her hands as she raised the carafe then caught the drip with a folded white cloth. Long fingers, short nails with no polish, a gold wedding band.

"You'll like our coffee," she said. "Everyone does. You look like you could use a good dose of it. I'll pour Ev's cup then leave you the rest of the pot."

Her eyes were restful like her voice, their color as soft as the easy green glow of the neon sign that had lit when he'd first hit town with the trucker.

"Did they get much rain in Salt Lake? Trav makes the Salt Lake City run twice a month. I'm guessing he picked you up there."

"It was raining hard," Frank said, his voice rougher than he would have wished.

"I'm glad. The winter was far too dry."

She'd said it as if she cared. About rain for people five hundred miles north. He felt something like a smile start deep in his gut, though he knew it would not surface.

The front door swung open again, then slammed shut. "Ran 'er bone-dry to bring you the business, Katie, m' love." The trucker shoved a wad of bills into the pocket of the white cook's apron the woman wore over her jeans, then yanked out the chair across from Frank and eased his heavy frame down.

"Better keep that diesel tank full for us back-road warriors, Kate. You met my silent friend?"

"Not really, Trav. No name." She filled the trucker's cup.

Trav took a swallow of coffee and set the cup back in its saucer with a clatter. "Then let me have the honor. Kate Prescott, meet Frank Vincenti. From somewhere east of Salt Lake, on his way to somewhere south of L.A. Frank, this here is Kate Newton Prescott. Crossing's named after her dad. Owned the place and ran the garage and business for years. We sure as hell missed the old man when he passed, but *not* his coffee." The trucker raised his cup in tribute.

At the next table a thin-faced woman lifted her cup too. "*Speaking* of coffee..."

"Pleased to meet you," Kate murmured, and turned away.

Kate. Nice name. Simple, clean, like her café. Like her life, probably.

The cook swung away from the grill. "Cheeseburger medium, French fries, beans on the side," he bellowed. "Mattie, will you get over here and pick up this order?"

An elderly man leaned out from the table near the door. "Could the missus have a pot of tea when you get a minute, Kate?"

"With a bit of lemon, dear, if you have it," his wife added as she tucked a stray curler back under a thin blue scarf.

A couple of teenagers got up from the counter and put money into the jukebox, and the cook yelled again, over the din. Frank watched the woman turn, touch the arm of the waitress, say something that must have been reassuring. The waitress smiled and moved toward the grill. Frank looked out the window.

Night was falling fast. He could barely make out the black silhouette of distant desert mountains and the ribbon of road that led toward them.

They've got racetrack roads in Nevada, man. Ramrod straight, sweetheart asphalt, mile after empty mile. Hell of a place to take a ride.

His kid brother had been right, at least about Nevada, Frank thought. But there would be no more races, not here, not anywhere else. Jesse was dead. It was over. He was free, Frank thought. Maybe in another few days he'd feel it as strongly as he knew it.

But damn it, Jesse. Why the hell didn't you ever listen?

By the time the chaos had quieted and Kate got a moment to breathe, Trav's table was empty. A whisper of disappointment settled over her, rare as a desert snowstorm and just as sudden. She cashed out the rest of the customers.

"Trav always was one to eat in a hurry," Mattie said over the din of the jukebox. "But that guy he had with him didn't even order except for coffee. Bet you he was on the run. Nice-looking fellow, but—"

Kate tossed the waitress a dishrag. "Mattie, it would help if your legs moved half as fast as your imagination."

"Okay, okay, I'm going. By the way, *Trooper MacMillan* said to say he'd see you on Sunday. No excuses." Kate rolled her eyes and Mattie chuckled. "Give him a chance, Kate. Everybody else has except for Miss Uptight White out there."

Mattie marched back to the dish room, leaving Kate to clear tables. Outside the window, Ev White stepped back from the cruiser then watched it head toward the stoplight. It would be quite a match, Kate thought. Mac, who fancied himself such a skirt-chaser, with Ev the straitlaced moralist. As odd a match as the one she'd made with Charlie.

A rock and roll chorus thundered from the jukebox, shaking the Saguaro's walls. The teenagers had turned up the volume again. Kate covered her ears and squeezed in behind the machine, her back pressed against the side window. She worked her way down.

But just as her fingers touched the knob, the music faded. She waited. Nothing. Kate groaned.

"Is there a problem?"

His voice was like suede. She froze just long enough to register the fact that her heart was hammering, then Kate peered out and up dusty black leather dress boots and long, dark-trousered legs.

She tried to stand. The back of her head caught smartly on the bottom edge of the windowsill.

The legs bent instantly.

"I'm okay." She reached up to rub her head, caught her sleeve on a screw and tore a jagged rip. "Oh, *damn*. There goes my last starched blouse." Kate looked into quicksilver eyes just inches from her own.

"Sorry I startled you."

"It wasn't you."

One dark eyebrow rose.

"Getting back in this corner was tough, but the jukebox needed fixing, like the screen door, the counter, any number of things around here." She stopped for a breath and moistened dry lips. "I could use one favor."

"Name it."

"Play a song so I can set the volume."

Seconds later a tone so mellow the volume hardly mattered flowed out from the speaker, Hank Williams's "I'm so Lonesome I Could Cry."

She wasn't lonesome, Kate thought. She had Bobby. And she'd had Charlie, too, if only for a little while.

Kate took her time fiddling with the volume control knob. She checked the connectors on the back of the jukebox and blew dust off the sill, then she pressed her back to the window and edged out. The glass was still warm. Mac had been right, the night wasn't cooling down.

Frank Vincenti was over at the counter with Mattie.

"That'll be twenty-nine dollars even with tax."

Frank opened his wallet, hesitated, then handed her a bill.

"You got anything smaller?" Mattie asked, fanning herself with the room registration card. "I hate to take a hundred dollar note this late. I'm low on change as it is."

"Sorry," he said. "That's all I have. My credit cards—"

"We don't take credit cards," Mattie snapped.

"Just keep it then."

"Keep the *whole*—"

"I'm not going anywhere for at least twelve hours. Take out an extra ten for your trouble. I'll collect the rest tomorrow."

Mattie managed a grudging smile; a thank-you was beyond her, Kate knew. "Number six at the end of the row. Did it up myself just yesterday."

Bo grunted. "It's the only room without a drippin' shower. Mattie ain't going to risk that ten."

Frank picked up the room key and slung a black leather backpack over his shoulder. Then he looked across the café, past the red vinyl stools at the counter, down toward the jukebox, toward Kate. He didn't smile, really. He just gave her a long, quiet look. Then he shouldered through the door.

The screen slammed behind him, jarring the last of the song. Bo went back to scraping the griddle. Mattie shut the cash register drawer. Kate stood still as stone.

Something had changed, she knew. Suddenly the night outside the big front window seemed deeper, the lingering smell of fried onions more pungent, the red-and-white checks on the tablecloths perfectly aligned.

Then the screen door slammed again, pulling her back to reality. The café filled with voices, the late dinner crowd. She had a business to run.

By eight o'clock the café had emptied, but Frank Vincenti had not returned. Maybe he wouldn't, Kate thought. As tired as he'd looked he'd probably gone straight to bed. Or maybe he was trying to conserve his cash. Without credit cards—

"It's so darn hot I hate to turn on the oven," Bo said. He stopped in the middle of trimming a pie and wiped his cheek with a forearm, leaving a smudge of flour.

Kate sighed in agreement as she worked the dough for tomorrow's yeast rolls. "Mattie," she called out, "go to the dish room and throw the switch on the rooftop cooler, would you?"

"Uh-huh." But the waitress kept wiping at the far countertop, her attention on the evening paper.

She glanced at Bobby, bent over his books at the back table. Another boy might be up at the house watching TV or buried in a comic book, but Bobby was there, attacking the math homework Ev *claimed* he'd been neglecting.

Kate leaned toward the cook and spoke in a lowered voice. "Bo, do *you* think I'm too easy on Bobby?"

The big man chuckled. "I wouldn't exactly call it *easy.* You ain't too heavy-handed with the rules, but you keep an eye out. Maybe too keen an eye, though."

"You're saying I'm overprotective? Oh, great. I'm overprotective *and* too permissive."

"You been listenin' to that old maid schoolteacher again."

"If Ev's an old maid, so am I," Kate said as she formed the dough into clovers. "We're both thirty-two, we went all through school together, and I'm not married, either."

"Not bein' married don't make a woman old and dried-up. 'Specially not if she's a widow."

Kate thought of Frank Vincenti, standing in the doorway, his eyes connecting with her own. Old and dried-up, heart turned to stone might just be safer. It had been a long time since a man like that had come to the crossing. A man so sure of himself he didn't need looks. *Though God knows he's got them,* Kate thought.

Mattie slid the paper down the counter. "Nothing's there."

"Nothin' 'bout what?" Bo asked.

"Our mysterious stranger. No car, no license number. And he didn't put any address on the room card. I thought there might be a Wanted article or something. I was going to ask Mac, only he left too quick. Maybe tomorrow at breakfast."

"Mattie Thompson, don't you *dare.*"

Hands on broad hips, Mattie rocked back on her heels. "Okay. But it sure is tempting. This is the first time I've ever seen you give a man a second glance."

"I haven't—"

"You were looking over your shoulder all the while Trav was here. And every time you go back to the dish room, you look out the door toward the units."

"I was wondering if he's going to come back for dinner, that's all. Coffee's not much for a man who's been on the road all day."

"All day and longer for all we know."

"You're *so* suspicious, Mattie."

"And *you're* a soft touch," Bo said. "Just remember, Kate, a hawk with a broken wing can still bite the hand that feeds it."

Kate felt the fine hairs beneath her braid stiffen. She shouldered the tray of rolls and headed toward the dish room. "Get *all* those crumbs out of the counter crevices, Mattie," she ordered from the doorway. "I'm going out back to turn on the cooler."

The stout woman groaned. "You're as laid-back as they come, Kate Prescott, till time for spring cleaning rolls around."

A moment later, as Kate crossed the threshold from the dish room, Frank Vincenti came through the front door. The few remaining customers quieted and turned the same way they had earlier. Mattie looked up from the counter; Bo, from the grill.

But he'd changed to denims as faded as her own and a worn chambray shirt not that much different from the local uniform. Kate shot her employees an I-told-you-so look. Mattie eyed Kate darkly and went back to her cleaning. Bo headed for the dish room with a load of pies.

"Still serving?" he asked.

Kate nodded. "There's stew on the back burner, tonight's special, or Bo can fix you something off the menu."

He drew a hand through curly, shower-damp hair and managed a look that could have been a smile if he'd let it, Kate thought. Then he headed for the back table where he'd sat with Trav. He saw Bobby and hesitated.

"It's okay. You can sit here," Bobby said. He rolled up a sheet of paper much too large to be math homework.

"Just don't let my son talk your leg off," she warned. As Kate wiped the table and set it, she watched Frank's eyes travel down the short list of entrées, stop on steaks, then move to the bottom of the menu: *Sorry, we can't accept credit cards.*

"Bo's stew is a favorite," Kate said. "It's the same price as the hamburger platter."

"It's real good," Bobby added. "I always ask for seconds."

"Fine. Bring me that. Please." He raised his water glass, his rolled sleeve pulling taut. Kate stared.

She knew what burns felt like. You couldn't work over a hot grill for long and not find out. But she didn't want to imagine what had caused the angry red mark that scarred the inner muscle of Frank Vincenti's forearm.

She brought him a salad and said it was part of the special, though it wasn't. She also brought twice the number of rolls and made sure they were piping hot. Then she stood over the stew pot, picking out the last big chunks of meat. Bo rolled his eyes but Kate ignored him.

"Refills are free after nine o'clock," she said to Frank when she brought the order. Such a clever promotion. Why hadn't she ever considered it before?

He declined more stew but questioned her about how far it was to L.A. and whether or not there'd be late-night truckers coming through.

"We're a little better than three hundred miles from the coast," Kate said, "but most of the regulars stay off the mountain after dark…and you've paid for the room till morning."

His eyes met hers briefly, then moved to stare out the window.

She filled his cup again, then quietly cleared the table and headed for the dish room.

Bobby tossed his pencil onto the table. "This dumb old stuff is boring. I hate these stupid story problems."

"You'll get it in time, kid."

"Not by tomorrow. We're gonna have a test. If I don't do real good, I might have to go to summer school. I'll have Miss White *again.*"

The small boy's freckled nose wrinkled in frustration. He had green eyes, his mother's eyes.

"I bet you know math," he said to Frank. "I bet you're real good."

It seemed like yesterday. Only he'd been the one with the earnest words, the one pushing. *School's important, Jesse.*

Bobby nudged the open book across the table. "Could you just take a look? Please?"

Frank's eyes had clouded but they began to clear as he studied the page. *If a train is traveling at sixty miles an hour…* Nobody travels by train anymore, Frank thought.

Half an hour later the café's overhead lights flickered, then dimmed. The boy didn't notice. His head was bent over his tablet where Frank had written another problem, one that would interest a nine-year-old kid. The café was empty except for him and Bobby, Kate and the cook she called Bo.

Then the lights went out altogether, the hum of the air conditioner dying with them, leaving only the glow from the sign out front. In the artificial twilight Frank watched Kate turn and reach for a flashlight on a high shelf.

He'd never seen a woman move the way she did. He'd watched her slip between the tables, bend over the counter, pick up dishes and set them down, and all with a supple grace that seemed to come to her as naturally as breathing. She was at ease in her body, he thought, the way he used to be when he fastened the harness across his chest and rode a new race car out onto an empty test track.

Bobby scrambled out of his chair. "I'll bring Bo the flashlight, Mom."

Over at the counter, she struck a match. Candlelight swept her hands as she moved toward his table. She set the candle down and the light traveled up her arm, her shoulder, the edge of her cheek. Flecks of gold had settled in her eyes.

"Bo's checking the fuse box," she said. "We should have the other circuit on in a minute."

She hesitated, then sat down in Bobby's chair and leaned back, away from the candle. He thought of an antique photograph, sepia trimmed in velvet.

"Thanks for helping Bobby," she said.

He nodded.

"I've been told he needs a better environment, more opportunity."

"He'll make his own chances for himself if you let him."

"*If* I let him?" She laughed and the sound was like the stroke of a feather. "You're the second person today to hint that I'm overprotective."

Overprotective? Could any child be protected too much?

A stack of pots rattled on the counter as the cook bumped past them and lumbered toward the table. "We're in trouble, Kate. I been up on the roof. That damn fool cooler's blown some kind of gasket. Smells like a junkyard up there. If I throw the circuit, it might start a fire."

"We knew it was only a matter of time. At least it's gone out now before the weather's hot every day."

"It ain't the cooler I'm worried about. There's melted wires. It don't look good. We got a full refrigerator and the rest of them pies to bake, not to mention tomorrow's breakfast."

"I could take a look," Frank said.

The cook's eyes narrowed. "A look ain't going to give us power."

"I could get things going, get you through till tomorrow."

Kate rubbed her temples. "At union prices plus double on overtime, including the forty-minute drive down from Summit City, I'd be grateful for *anything* you could do."

Frank stood, and the cook stepped aside, though grudgingly.

Kate rose, too. "I'll comp your dinner for tonight. And breakfast tomorrow morning if you decide to stay for it."

If he decided...

In the distance, the long, lonely call of a whistle sounded as a semi slowed for the stoplight. A trucker heading in for gas, maybe a southbound night driver...

The woman moved. Framed in the window, the green light draping her shoulders, she seemed almost an apparition.

"Dinner was good," Frank said quietly. "I'll look forward to breakfast."

California could wait.

An hour later, after considerable stomping around on the roof and numerous muffled curses from Bo, the lights inside the café came back on.

The back screen slammed and Bobby ran in. "Frank and Bo are taking the cooler motor across the street to Grandpop's garage," he said. "Frank thinks he can fix it. Bo ain't so sure."

"Bo *isn't* so sure."

"Yes, ma'am. I finished my homework, can I go help?"

"It's late."

"Aw, *Mom.*"

"Quarter of an hour, not a minute longer. Then up to the house for your bath. I've got to stay late and work on the books. Tell Bo I'll take care of the pies."

An hour passed, then two. She'd phoned the house at ten to remind Bobby to lock the door and get to bed. Half an hour later Bo had crossed the street to tap on the glass. She'd pointed toward the pies cooling on the counter. He'd nodded, then rolled his eyes toward the garage across the street. Kate shrugged and Bo turned and stalked off, heading for the trailer behind it.

It was close to midnight when she closed the books. Across the street, the light in the garage still burned.

Kate gathered up the register tapes, the stack of bills that had to be paid and the other pile that could wait, and closed them all in the account book. Then she put out clean dish towels and unplugged the coffeepot. One cup left. She poured it into a mug.

Before she could change her mind, she cut a wedge of the still-warm pie and put it and the coffee on a tray. Fork, napkin, two packets of sugar, cream—an order she repeated a hundred times a day, yet she had to concentrate to get it right.

Kate balanced the tray and locked up the Saguaro. From across the road a warm breeze carried the faint sounds of sad country music on Pop's old radio.

Was that the reason he was running? she wondered. A woman?

The music was just loud enough to cover her footsteps as Kate pushed open the door to the garage's office.

He'd taken off his shirt. Sweat gleamed, accentuating the muscles of his back, his broad shoulders, the dark hair that curled at the back of his neck. Kate stood perfectly still.

"I...brought you something to eat," she said finally.

He turned around. A small silver bird tattooed on his left shoulder seemed to move as he moved, as though taking flight. He reached for his shirt.

His eyes held hers, but at arm's length. Kate felt like an intruder. And that stare. As if he were saying, *Don't you know a loner when you see one, lady?*

He pulled a stool up to the desk. "Sit down," he said.

She hesitated.

"Please ... sit down. I'm not used to seeing women around a garage, that's all."

"Is that what you do? Work in a garage?"

"Sometimes." He picked up the mug of coffee and took a swallow.

If his tone was evasive, his eyes were not. Kate felt them bore into her. "The pie is homemade," she said as he reached for the fork. "I hope you like apple. We do all our own pies and other desserts, also dinner rolls. We'd do bread, too, but we use so much, we'd be baking night and day."

She paused for breath, and he glanced up at the old round-faced clock over the doorway. "Looks like you work night and day as it is. When do you sleep?"

"Now ... soon." Her mouth was dry again. She should have brought coffee for herself. And there was nothing to do with her hands.

As if reading her mind, he slid the mug across the desk. She hesitated, then touched her lips where his had been, inhaling the lingering smell of after-shave. Something exotic, expensive. She drank quickly, then passed the mug back.

Frank went on eating.

"Did you have any luck with the motor?"

"It will get you through the night."

More silence.

"Do you live in L.A. or are you going there just for a visit?"

His last forkful of pie hovered. "I've never been to Los Angeles."

"There's a lot to see. Disneyland. Universal Studios."

"I'm going to the ocean."

"That, too. The sand, the beach, it's a great place for a vacation."

"I'm not vacationing. I have an errand. It has to do with a promise I made to my brother."

Not to a woman. "Does your brother live there?"

She watched him struggle, as if the answer were a barbell he'd pushed halfway off his chest but couldn't move higher.

"My brother is dead."

"I'm sorry," she said. She was quiet for a moment. "*Pacific* means *making peace.* Perhaps you'll find it when you get there."

"Maybe. It doesn't matter."

It's the only thing that matters, Kate wanted to say. She looked out the dirty window of the old garage, across the street to the cactus sign, the café, the motel, the house on the hill, its single light burning into the desert's darkness. If she closed her eyes, she would still see the picture in detail. She'd done it a thousand times when she'd been away at school, then at Edwards Air Force Base with Charlie. It had carried her through. She did not have to go to the ocean or anywhere else to find peace. It was here, in never-changing Newton's Crossing, and it always would be.

When she looked back, Frank, too, was staring out the window. "Where will you go after L.A.?" she asked him.

"I don't know."

"You must be pretty good with your hands—you rescued that motor. There are lots of things we need done around here."

"I'm not looking for a job."

"No. But if you'd like to stay on for a while . . ."

"I'll be pulling out in the morning, right after I seat this motor." He gave the flywheel a spin.

Kate stood up. "Of course. It was good to meet you. Have a restful night."

She considered extending a hand to shake his, then thought better of it. She moved toward the door. He didn't call her back.

Chapter Two

The sharp morning sunlight hurt Kate's eyes. Why didn't Ev just *go?* The teacher shaded her own eyes and leaned out the open car window.

"I'm not one to interfere, Kate, but when it comes to my students I have to speak up."

"Bobby's got a good head on his shoulders."

"He needs stability. He's not going to get it out here with all these *itinerants* hanging around. If you want to stay in the restaurant business, why not do it in Summit City? You could get a nice little house like mine in the suburbs, let Bobby have friends his own age, enroll him at one of the better schools."

"Ev, I like the special mix of ranchers' kids, isolated boys and girls like Bobby, Hispanics and Indians that go to our old school. And you must, too, or else why did you go back there to teach? And as for selling the Saguaro, you know I couldn't do that."

"*Wouldn't* sell, that's the word. You're tied to the past and you're holding Bobby back there with you. Kate—"

"Mom! Come and see, I got Lady's water dish working."

"Get your books, Bobby," Kate said sharply. "And hurry. Miss White is waiting."

"Yes, ma'am."

Bobby shuffled off, the old yellow Lab following, just as a state truck full of highway workers pulled into the parking lot.

A long-haired, slack-faced young man dressed in tattered denims jumped to the ground. The dog looked back and growled.

Ev glared. "As I was saying—"

"I promise I'll think about it," Kate said as she headed for the café's door.

Bobby came out and they met halfway. She bent down and straightened his collar. "I'm sorry I was sharp."

"It's okay, Mom."

"When you get home, you can show me the watering machine."

"It's a siphon, Mom. That guy in number six helped me fix it."

"Bobby, I've told you—"

"Frank's not a stranger anymore. He's a customer. And he knows a lot. I bet he knows as much as Grandpop did."

Ev gunned the engine and Bobby sprinted toward the car.

"Wear your seat belt, young man," Kate called out, knowing her reminder was superfluous. Evelyn White obeyed *all* the rules, and she made sure everybody else did, too.

Ev waved and Kate waved back. The car moved toward the intersection, hit the highway and headed around the base of the mountain. Maybe Ev was right about Bobby's environment. How would her son ever learn not to talk to strangers when she herself did it daily?

She had watched the car and the road too long. The deep vee cleft of Rock Top Mountain, shrouded in shadow, beckoned.

In her memory Kate heard again the *boom* of the exploding fighter jet, the sound that had hit the bottom of her stomach just before the air turned to fire, her life to ashes. *You married the wrong woman, Charles.* If her husband had chosen someone like Ev, he'd have lived by the rules of ordinary men, instead of making his own rules and then dying by them.

Or maybe not. Maybe a rigid woman instead of an accepting one would have made no difference.

A hot wind blew across Kate's face. Somewhere inside the café, glass shattered.

Bo had the scruffy young highway worker by the collar, pushing him out the door. "If I say you don't eat, you don't eat, little buddy. This ain't no bikers' pit stop. We got a clean place here. Nobody cusses at the ladies."

The foreman stepped between Bo and the man. "Easy, big fella. The dude's a temporary, he won't be back." The foreman caught the man roughly by the arm and hauled him toward the truck. "Sorry, Kate," he said as he passed her.

Bo headed for the dish room. Kate followed, signaling Mattie to tend to the customers.

The big man was trembling. "Aw, Kate, you know how it is. I couldn't let him act like some sorry excuse for a human being, not in front of Mattie. I had to pretend a little."

"You fooled me. I could have sworn that *he* was the one feeling nervous."

"Yeah...maybe. Guess I stood up for Mattie for once."

"You could take good care of Mattie all the time if you wanted to, Bo."

The big man shrugged and looked away for a moment. Then Bo's soft brown eyes came back, as much a contrast to his sun-weathered face as the motorcycle life had been to his nature, Kate thought.

"You want I should make the run into town a little early?"

"I'd appreciate that." Kate wanted to add more. *The crossing's as good a place as any to find yourself, Bo.*

The back door closed and a moment later Mattie stuck her head in the dish room doorway. "We're low on eggs."

"Bo's gone for supplies."

Mattie smoothed her apron and brushed wisps of black hair off her wide cheekbones. "I don't know what got into him," she said as she turned away.

He wants to earn your respect. Kate thought of the day two years ago when the couple had ridden in on Bo's motorcycle looking for work, tired, dirty, wind-swept, but Mattie with pride enough for both of them. It had made Kate look past the woman's tattered clothing, Bo's rough hands and rangy gray ponytail. She'd never been sorry.

Moments later a ladder hit the side of the café outside the front window, followed by footsteps crossing the roof. Kate glanced up for a second, then scooped scrambled eggs onto a big plate. "Go on and eat before we get busy, Mattie. You haven't had breakfast all week."

"Bo would say I could stand to skip more than breakfast," Mattie grumbled. "Though he should talk. Good thing he's not up there with Frank. He'd be putting one of his big feet through the roof any minute."

Kate didn't respond. There wasn't time to argue with Mattie this morning or to try to suggest that maybe she shouldn't be quite so hard on Bo.

The footsteps moved again, then stopped. She thought of the man above her, the tall, solid build, the strong, quiet face. And something else, a kind of tension just beneath the surface, something she felt in him more than saw. It was like the tightening of the air on the mesa that warned a storm was brewing . . . but she loved the desert rain, the jagged lightning, the deep roll of thunder—

"You're burning the bacon."

Kate grabbed a cooking fork. Frank Vincenti would be gone before the morning was over. Just as well. She had customers to feed and burned bacon was not on the menu.

* * *

Frank had just crossed the stretch of hard sand between the motel and café when a battered blue pickup pulled up to the dish room door. Bo cut the engine and it shimmied to a stop.

"Need help unloading?" Frank asked the cook.

"Ain't you afraid you'll get all messed up?"

Frank hooked the black suit coat over the truck's side mirror and tossed his backpack onto the faded hood.

Bo shoved a box into his arms. "You can help if you don't dawdle. I got to get in there to the omelet crowd. *Them's* payin' customers."

"I have no intention of allowing the lady to buy my breakfast, or last night's dinner."

"Well, ain't that hoity-toity. I can see you're feelin' just as independent as you were last night when you said you didn't need no help with the motor."

"I'm *feeling* like hitching a ride on the first truck out, before something else breaks down around here."

"That's good. Kate don't need no more hangers-on."

They made three trips, dumping the groceries in the dish room where Bo insisted that Mattie would find them when she got back from her break. Then the big cook finally quit grumbling and tied on his apron.

"The *man* says you can turn the cooler on," Frank heard Bo mutter as he returned with his backpack. Then Kate came through the door to the dish room.

For an instant her eyes were as green and warm as the flag on the Indy track raceway. A pump of the old adrenaline shot through Frank. She handed him an envelope.

"Mattie took her ten. The rest is there, all ones and fives—I hope you don't mind. And late as it is, I still owe you breakfast."

"You don't owe me anything."

"You fixed the motor. Bo says—"

"That you don't need hangers-on."

"It wouldn't be like that. It's not that way with Bo and Mattie."

He slid the backpack higher on his shoulder. The lacquered box in the bottom zippered pocket shifted.

"I'll have coffee and eggs," Frank said. "As soon as a trucker headed south rolls in, I'll be on my way."

He'd leave payment for dinner and breakfast by his plate, Frank thought as he chose a stool at the far end of the counter.

He took his time eating. She'd glance at him, find him watching her, look away. *Kate don't need a man the way women alone sometimes do,* Bo had said, adding that she still wore the ring to keep them away. So her job offer of last night had come from someplace else, Frank thought, from something intrinsic to her nature.

She greeted every man, woman and child who came into the café. She'd ask about kids, jobs, plans for summer vacation. She knew who was out of work and whose boy was due home from college for spring break. Frank figured she knew more about the people she served than anybody had ever known about him in his life.

He could appreciate that kind of caring. Maybe envy its recipients.

Then she stooped to retrieve a napkin she'd dropped and he found himself appreciating something else— the way her jeans hugged the curve of her hips.

She rose and caught him staring. He thought she colored, but it could have been the light. She went back to her work. He nursed his coffee.

Half an hour later the counter and the tables had emptied. Frank swiveled around to look out the front window and watch for a truck with California tags. He saw, instead, a blue-and-white Nevada State Highway Patrol car pulling into the parking lot.

The screen door banged shut behind the trooper, who hung his hat behind the door and glanced at the black leather backpack, then across the café.

Frank put on his dark glasses.

Kate came out of the dish room. "Hi, Mac. You're awfully late this morning."

The trooper cleared his throat. "Got tied up on the interstate, Kate. Important business."

The stack of plates Bo carried hit the counter with a clatter. Kate frowned at the noise. "I hope nobody was hurt, Mac."

"Hurt? Oh, no. Driver was a little shook up. Took awhile to clean things up."

"Oh, yeah," Bo said. "I heard it on the radio. Guy dumped his chickens goin' up the hill. The whole darn highway was covered with feathers and chicken, uh, droppings."

"Bo—"

"Yes, ma'am. I'll be going out back to check that blown outlet now." Bo eyed the trooper as he passed him. "Must've been somethin', chasing them birds."

MacMillan's face lit brighter than the blinking light at the crossroads. He glared at Bo's back, then down the counter.

Frank watched the window, pretending he hadn't heard the exchange and couldn't care less anyway.

Kate set a plate of French toast and a jug of syrup down on the table near the door and waved the trooper toward it. "Mac, listen to me," she said. "About Sunday—"

"Kate, I've got bad news. Potter's been down in Vegas for that new training class and wants to stay over for the weekend. I owe him a favor, and he'll have to cover for me when I go week after next. Take a rain check?"

"Mac—"

"Or, if you're willing, maybe we could have a late supper. Pizza, buffalo wings...I could pick up a video. I know this hot store in Summit City." Mac grinned and reached for the syrup.

Kate laughed uneasily. "No, Mac. I don't think I'd like—"

"Come on, Kate. They're a big turn-on. You'll never know unless you give it a try."

At the other end of the counter, Frank gripped his own cup. *The lady doesn't care for pornography, man.*

"Mac, there's something you need to understand. I don't think I'm ready to date."

And when she's ready it's a damn sure sight it won't be you.

She'd been twisting the ring on her finger. Mac-Millan put down his fork and covered her hands. Kate tried to draw away, but he held them fast.

Frank's gut clinched into the old, hard knot. *You can take him out with a single punch, son. Go on and do it the Vincenti way.* His father's voice egged him on, even from the grave.

"Let's go on just being friends, Mac," Kate said to the trooper. "Finish your breakfast, now, before it gets cold."

His eyes on Kate, Mac sopped up syrup with the last of his French toast, chewed, then glanced down the counter at Frank. He chewed again and swallowed hard. A thread of syrup spun off his raised fork and dribbled down the front of his starched blue shirt.

"You want something, mister?"

The corner of Frank's mouth twitched. He didn't answer.

The trooper took a swallow of coffee, wiped his mouth and stood up.

Frank's muscles went from tense to rigid as the man started toward him. The trooper stopped barely a foot away and leaned against the counter.

"You have something you want to say to the state of Nevada, buddy?"

From behind dark lenses, Frank watched. The trooper's eyes darted over Frank's face, looking for a place to land.

Frank took off his glasses. The trooper's gaze locked on his.

Then the screen door banged closed behind a trucker.

"*Must* you slam that door?" Kate's voice rang out.

"If y'all'd get it fixed..."

Frank was standing now, eye to eye with Mac-Millan.

"Well?" the trooper said.

"You've got syrup on your shirt, *sir.*"

"What the . . . ?" MacMillan looked down at the sticky dark trail that stopped just short of his belt. He grabbed a napkin and rubbed at the stain till bits of white tissue shredded and stuck fast..

"Oh, damn."

"Gotta use water," the trucker said as he settled at the window table. "Cloth rag, too, not paper."

Mac grabbed the dishcloth Kate offered and stalked off toward the rest room.

When the trooper came back a few minutes later, Frank and the trucker were deep in conversation.

"Who is this guy, Kate?" Mac asked as she filled his cup.

"His name is Frank Vincenti."

"What's he driving? Where's he from? You get his plate on the reg card?"

"He's just a drifter, Mac. He hitched in with Trav last night."

"Looks like he'll be leaving that way, too." Mac's voice had risen and the men looked his way. "You let me know anytime any of these guys make trouble. You let me—"

"Frank!" Bo hollered from the dish room doorway. "Give me a hand, will you? I want to be sure I got this outlet wired right."

Mac shot Kate a questioning look.

"Frank helped us out last night when the power failed," she said. "It was the cooler motor again."

"You could have called me."

Bo let out a snort, then coughed and pretended to examine his nails.

Mac leaned a shade closer to Kate. "You call *me* next time, Kate. I'm a real fixer-upper. I can—"

"That won't be necessary," Frank said at the trooper's elbow. "The lady has hired me to work around the place. I'll be taking care of whatever needs fixing for a while."

"I . . . offered him the job last night," Kate said.

"You're sure about this?"

"Oh, yes, Mac," she said.

Frank smiled. It almost hurt, his jaw had been set so firmly for so many days. She had looked at him as she spoke, not the trooper. And her voice had held that same curious mix of softness and fire that he'd seen last night when she'd torn her blouse . . . a crisp white blouse, like the one she wore now, snowy against the light expanse of skin that was wide at her throat, narrower where it plunged toward full breasts. "Where's the outlet, Bo?" he heard himself ask.

"Uh, left of the sink in the dish room, Frank."

The trucker rose to pay for his coffee. The trooper reached for his hat and his eye fell on the black backpack and suit jacket hanging next to it.

"Guess your new handyman won't need a ride west after all," the trucker called out to Kate. He chuckled and eyed MacMillan.

Mac took one look at Kate's crimson face, smashed his hat onto his head and stalked toward the door. He slammed the screen so hard it bounced twice before it closed.

The cruiser took off in a cloud of dust that threw gravel so high it hit the front window.

"He busts that glass, you make him pay, Kate," Bo yelled from the dish room.

"That'll be the day," the trucker said on his way out.

"Mac's out of sorts," Kate said as Bo headed out from the dish room. "I, on the other hand, have never felt better."

"Kate—"

"Just don't say it, Bo Thompson. Don't you dare say a thing to spoil this for me."

Half an hour later, after Frank had changed and returned to the café and Mattie had returned from her break, Kate sat down at the back table and handed him the list.

"I've put things down in order from most to least important," she said. "Start with those leaky faucets in the units, then wash the windows and put up the screens so we can open up on cooler days. Now, about your wages—"

"Room and board if you can spare the unit." He took the pencil from her and began to make a list of his own.

"That's not enough. The weekly room rate is only one-fifty, and your meals will run less than that."

"Last I heard, window washers draw minimum wage."

"You're not a window washer, Mr. Vincenti."

The pencil snapped in two. A piece flew up and his hand shot out. "Call me Frank. Please."

"Pop used to catch flies like that."

"Quick reflexes . . . are useful."

"Yes, well . . . just let me know if you need anything, or speak to Mattie or Bo. And you can come in for lunch whenever you're ready."

He tore off a corner of the page. "Ask your cook to pick up these parts. I'll rebuild that motor properly since I'm going to be around awhile."

She studied the paper, avoiding his eyes. "How long is 'a while'?"

He took a long time answering. So long that she wished she hadn't asked. When she looked up, his eyes were hard.

"I have a lot of anger toward my brother. It doesn't seem right to carry that to California with his ashes."

"Your West Coast errand?"

Frank nodded.

"How did he die?" she asked gently.

Again his answer took time, but when it came it was sharp and direct, almost a curse. *"Car wreck."*

She nodded. "I know about losing someone you love, suddenly, senselessly. My husband was killed five years ago when his jet fighter crashed. Charlie was a test pilot. He...took a chance."

Frank started to respond but she rose, closing him off. "We'll take it a day at a time," she said. "You can let me know when you're ready to leave and we'll settle up."

"I'll do your room at the end of the week," Mattie said as Frank passed her. "Clean linens and such."

He nodded, then headed out.

Mattie waited till he was out of sight. "You've gone and done it now, Kate Prescott. You don't know a thing about that guy. He could be an escapee from some prison or mental hospital."

"Oh, *Mattie.*"

"Any man who raises the hackles on the back of a law enforcement officer the way he raises them up on

Mac has got something to hide, you mark my words. You should have found out what it was before you hired him. Now you'll never know."

"When the time is right and he's ready, he'll tell me."

"You're awfully trusting, Kate." Mattie crossed the floor to the table and picked up the empty coffee mugs, then waited for Kate to meet her eyes. "You're trusting and patient and far too accepting. Think about yourself for a change."

Kate smiled to herself. The creak of the hinges on the garage doors across the street had sounded like music. Outside, the two men stood side by side looking in at the empty bays. Bo, hands shoved into his pockets, kicked at the edge of the lift, then looked up and said something to Frank.

The taller man threw back his head and laughed. The sound of it carried across the road, rich and full and as sweeping as the desert horizon.

Kate's spirits soared. "Who says I'm *not* thinking about myself?"

Mattie shot her a wary look and slowly shook her head.

Bo finished the lunch prep early and left with a sandwich and a soda that Kate knew were intended for Frank. Then Mac came in, still fit to be tied, and she was glad Frank hadn't come for lunch.

At two, the café emptied. Kate dragged in the dish room stepladder, climbed up and began sliding dusty red-checked fabric off the big curtain rods.

Mattie groaned. "I suppose you want them washed *and* ironed."

"Yes, thank you."

"At least it's only once a year. I'll throw them in the washer after the towels and do them up tonight during 'Wheel of Fortune.'"

The café stayed blissfully quiet after Mattie had gone. Kate dusted the curtain rods and braces, washed the sills, then finally started on the glass itself.

The strong smell of vinegar, the sound of squeaking newspaper, the clearer view with each new wipe, all filled Kate with peace. Nothing had changed. It was spring again at the crossing, and she was washing the very same windows she'd washed since she'd been old enough to climb the stepladder.

Kate moved the ladder to the big front window and shifted her buckets. Then she stood stone still.

Frank stood on the other side of the window, a squeegee in one hand, a bucket in the other, a towel hanging out of his left hip pocket. She stared at him and he stared back.

She did the only thing she could think of. She reached down and came up with a sponge full of water and slopped it across the window just below his chin. Water ran in rivulets down the glass between them. She bent to pick up the balled newspaper.

On the other side of the window, when she came up, the squeegee came down. His tall form blurred into a moving swath of jeans, white T-shirt and olive-toned skin.

Kate worked fast. Frank worked faster. With methodical strokes, he stripped the dust and dried bugs off the window, flipped the squeegee and pulled the rubber blade down the glass.

She had to stop now and then to climb the ladder, but he was tall enough to reach the topmost corner just by stretching. Up the ladder, down the ladder, each time she passed in front of his eyes, she tried to avoid them. Then once she failed and found that she needn't have bothered. His gaze slid over hers as though she weren't there, as though *he* weren't there, but miles away.

He would be soon, she thought.

But there was a streak in the middle of the window. She wiped it, then turned the newspaper and wiped again.

Under Frank's towel, the smudge vanished.

Their hands paused on opposite sides, touching except for the glass. The muscle tensed in his shoulder. She thought of the tattooed bird, moving beneath his shirt.

Kate pulled her hand away to tuck an errant wisp from her braid behind one ear. His eyes followed the movement, then slid to her face and stilled.

Wherever he'd been, he was back. He looked at her openly, with a penetrating steadiness that demanded she not look away.

They worked in silent harmony. He waited while she moved the ladder. She paused when he had to go over a high corner again. She pushed the sponge side to side. He matched her stroke with the squeegee. Her arm muscles stretched, his tightened and released. She grew warm with the effort. A bead of sweat rolled down his temple.

They finished the last window, the one next to the door. Kate opened the screen and leaned out. "Want something cold to drink?"

Frank made a move to accept, then hesitated. "Maybe later," he said. He squinted into the afternoon sun, then pulled dark glasses out of his hip pocket and put them on.

Kate turned away, disappointed. He was keeping his distance. Why? She thought of Mattie's warning.

At three she'd just finished rinsing the lettuce when Mattie came back from her afternoon break. "Did you start the towels?" Kate asked.

"Uh-huh. Should be about done. You want to fold and deliver? I'll do the salads for dinner."

She'd hoped to get a start on reorganizing the pantry, but Mattie's offers to do dinner salad prep were few and far between, so Kate took the master key ring off the hook behind the register and headed out back.

The sand in the parking lot could use grading, she noticed as she crossed to the units. Another new crack was working its way up the adobe wall near Number two, and the rain gutters needed patching and paint. She'd add them to Frank's job list as soon as she got back to the dish room.

Outside Unit six, the old yellow Lab lay curled up under the window. Kate brushed flaking paint off the red metal patio chair and set the clean towels down on it, then stooped to stroke the dog. Lady opened one rheumy eye and sighed, then went back to dreaming.

Beyond, water slopped into the dog's dish. The siphon that Bobby had been fooling with for more than a week actually seemed to be working. She thought of her son and warmed.

He's not a stranger, Mom. He knows a lot.

She glanced toward the garage, wondered what Frank was doing, then gathered up the towels and knocked on the motel room door. No answer, of course. But she heard the sound of water. Had one of the pipes rusted out again? She turned the passkey quickly and stepped into the room.

He had the faucets running full blast. Except for the towel wrapped around his waist, Frank was completely naked.

Kate started to back out of the room, but his eyes met hers in the mirror. Everything about him stilled.

"I thought you were working in the garage," she managed to say.

He leaned over to shut off the faucets. "I was doing fine till I dumped half a can of screen paint down the leg of my jeans."

"I... brought you clean towels."

"Thanks, I just used the last one." In the mirror he indicated the knot at his waist.

Her eyes went to his stomach, flat as the glass that reflected it, marked by a thin line of dark hair that disappeared into the towel. She jerked her eyes up—he was watching her, watching in the mirror as she watched him. Heat rushed to Kate's face.

She turned abruptly and set the towels on the worn beige bedspread drawn neatly over the sagging mattress. His suit hung in the small open closet next to his backpack. His wallet, watch and key sat on the desk. No phone. No TV. Only the knotty pine walls and the new beige curtains lent warmth to the sparsely furnished room. *She could offer so little.*

"I could run those jeans through the wash," she said quickly. "It's no trouble. I'll use the motel machine."

"I'd appreciate that." He bent over the sink to wring out the fabric.

He'd need a haircut soon, Kate thought, staring at the back of his neck. She'd get Ev to give him one next time she came to do Bobby's. Or maybe she'd do it herself. She'd hung around Ev's mother's beauty shop, too, as a child, hadn't she?

Frank passed her the dripping jeans, his face unreadable.

"Do you have something else to put on?"

"Only my suit. I left in a hurry." The towel around his waist shifted. He reached for the knot.

Kate's eyes snapped back to his face. She thought she saw the whisper of a smile play across his mouth. His eyes roamed her face. Kate remained silent and utterly still, as she had years ago when the old blind prospector, a friend of her father's, had asked to "see" her face with his fingers.

"It'll take about an hour for these to wash and dry," she said when she found her voice. "I'm sure you could use a break."

He nodded as she backed toward the door. "Is your cook going to town tomorrow? I'd be grateful if he'd pick up some things."

"I'll tell Bo to check with you before he leaves."

Outside on the walk, Kate closed her eyes against the strong sunlight. The day had grown hot. She could almost imagine that spring had skipped the crossing completely, that they'd passed into summer without her even noticing.

But tonight was supposed to turn cool again. Things would be back to normal, inside her head and out.

Chapter Three

It was late when Frank locked the garage and crossed the road for dinner. Kate was busy with a busload of kids whose team had just won their first baseball game. He had a few moments undetected to watch her work, watch her joke with the teens, move around the café. She was quick but never frantic, efficient but never abrupt. He caught her eye. She smiled and nodded. Then Mattie was at his table to take his order.

The noise from the jukebox was deafening. He was glad when the song had ended. Then Bobby slid into the opposite chair. Thin shoulders, a brush of unruly, sandy-colored hair, and all that energy...so much like Jesse it made his throat hurt.

"I did okay on the test, I think. Won't know till tomorrow." Bobby grinned and unrolled the paper he'd brought, then anchored two corners with the salt and pepper, a third with Frank's coffee mug, a fourth with his elbow.

Rock Top Mountain Regional Soap Box Derby Rally. Junior Division. Frank smiled wryly as he glanced over at the boy's drawing. He'd come halfway across the country to get away from racing, but in one form or another it was not going to turn loose of him quite as easily as he'd let go of it.

"What do you think?" Bobby asked. "Will it work? I was thinking maybe you'd have suggestions, like with Lady's water dish."

Frank broke another roll and used half to soak up the last of his gravy. "When's the race?"

"Not till April, but there are qualifying ones before that. I figure I've got just enough time to finish and get into the first one *if* Mom signs off on the permission form."

"Have you asked her yet?"

Bobby shook his head. "She doesn't like Rock Top Mountain. That's where they hold the race."

"I'll be gone by April, kid. I don't think I ought to get involved."

Bobby lifted his elbow and a corner of the sheet rolled forward. "Okay." He shrugged and reached for the anchoring cup.

"Maybe . . . just one thing." Frank took the pencil from the boy's shirt pocket and drew two light lines on the sketch. He tapped their intersection. "Move as much as you can of the body forward, ahead of its widest point."

Bobby studied the sketch, then looked up, his eyes bright. "Hey, *thanks!*"

He glanced toward his mother, her back to them as she stacked small cereal boxes on a high shelf. Bobby leaned across the table, his hands to his mouth to shield a whisper. "Don't tell my mom, okay? I figure if I just go slow, it'll be like it was with Pop and my dad. Like it is with Mattie and Bo. Nothing *they* do worries her." Bobby slouched down in his chair. *"Women,"* he muttered.

Frank laughed out loud and Kate glanced their way. Bobby quickly rolled up the paper.

Just go slow? Good advice in most situations, Frank thought, especially for someone like himself.

The café had been closed for half an hour. Bo had gone back to the trailer and Bobby up to the house. Kate lingered, filling the toothpick holder, putting out a new box of matchbooks. Dinner had been chaotic and she needed time to wind down, she had told herself. Now even the pumps across the street were quiet, though the light was still on in the garage.

She wouldn't cross the street again. She'd done that last night. Then this afternoon, she'd barged into his room. She would head up to the house, as usual, climb into bed with a book and read till she fell asleep.

Kate stepped outside into night air that had finally cooled enough to carry the fragrance of winter-washed sand, creosote and the first cactus flowers. Spring had arrived on schedule after all, and with it, her usual restlessness. But it was worse this year. It was as though she'd left something undone, a light still on, a pot still simmering.

The full moon she'd promised Bobby for their Saturday night horseback ride was nowhere in sight.

There was only the green glow of the Saguaro's sign, the light up the hill on the porch of the house, the one in the window across the street.

A coyote called, waited for an answer that did not come, then called again. Kate shivered, the lonely sound sinking into her bones.

The light across the street went out and the front door of Pop's garage opened. Kate stepped back, into the shadows.

He was crossing the street, headed straight for the café's door. Her heart started up a crazy pounding. But he stopped at the edge of the parking lot underneath the cactus sign.

"Kate?"

The resonance of his voice in the still, clear air drew her forward.

"Sorry I frightened you," he said.

"I'm rarely afraid. I'm not afraid now."

Perhaps you should be, he might have said as the shadow of his body stretched out behind him to make him seem even taller. Kate felt a shiver of awareness. She moved forward carefully, as though walking toward the edge of an arroyo.

"Mattie's convinced that you're some sort of criminal." She tried to laugh, more to cover her own disquietude than anything. "*Are* you some sort of criminal?"

A quick flash lit his eyes. "I've never broken the law."

His gaze slid down the dusty road and rose slowly toward the starlit night sky. Kate waited, ready to do what she'd done all her life. Listen, understand, accept.

"We can sit out on the porch and talk if you'd like to walk up to the house," she offered.

"Yes. If you're sure."

"I'm sure."

She matched his pace as they climbed the railroad-tie steps toward the low stone house on the hill. Once, the soft cotton sleeve of his shirt brushed across her bare arm; once, their shoulders touched. Nothing more but enough to give the restlessness Kate had been feeling a name, *his* name.

On the porch she indicated the cane-backed rocker rather than the wicker settee. "I'll just be a minute," she said.

Inside the house, the low lamplight beside Bobby's bed streaked his soft brown hair a rich honey, then moved on to shadow the dimple in his chin that always reminded her of Charles. One thin arm was curled around a book. *Wheels for Home Projects.* Too like his father, Kate thought with a sigh. Fascinated by anything mechanical.

Kate switched off the light and bent down to kiss her son. Awake, he'd insist on being too old for good-night kisses. All too soon he really would be.

She pushed open the screen door, carrying a tray. "Would you like a drink?"

Frank held the bottle up to the porch light and blew dust off the label. "Old, but very good."

"Pop would be pleased you noticed. He was as proud of his hoarded bourbon as he was of those tools you've been using, this house, the crossing..."

"My own father had an intimate relationship with liquor...while he was alive." Frank set the bottle on

the wide porch floorboards and accepted the glass of
water Kate offered.

"How long has your father been gone?"

He set the glass down and picked up a baseball that
Bobby had left in a glove. He tossed the ball from
hand to hand, weighing it as though weighing her
question, his answer. "My father died twelve years
ago. I'd finished up at MIT and been out on my own
for a while."

"Pop died after Bobby and I came back," Kate
said. "It's been four years. He had a bad heart, he
wouldn't slow down. My parents were older. I was a
late-life child. Mother died when I was ten." Kate
sipped her water.

"You sound . . . reconciled."

He tossed the ball to her and Kate caught it, warming her hand where his had been. Down the hill, beyond the buildings, the red stoplight at the intersection
blinked on and off in a rhythm as timeless as anything she could remember. Kate set aside the ball and
pulled her jean-clad knees up to hug them.

"I learned long ago that things just happen. Life.
Places. People. It's best to accept. Down deep things
stay the same. There's comfort in that."

Frank stood. *Not for me,* his eyes seemed to say. "I
never really knew my mother, but I'm sure I would
have accepted her if I'd had the chance. She left after
Jesse was born."

"Your father's drinking?"

"That. And other things." He turned away and
spread his hands wide on the worn wooden porch
railing. He leaned out over it into the night. Stars, so
many of them, seemed to fall about his shoulders, and

darkness hovered, black except for a pair of head-lights coming toward the crossroads. Frank bowed his head.

"I hope you're wrong about change," he said, his voice edged with agony. "I hope to God *I've* changed."

She was standing, then, her arms slipping gently around his body, her hands coming to rest in the center of his chest. She leaned her cheek against his back.

In the circle of her embrace, Frank felt his body empty of all the old tension and pause for a moment, suspended.

Then slowly he began to fill up again, fill with something new, something elusive.

Her palms pressed lightly against his chest. Her cheek, her breasts, were warm against his back. The fullness in his body began to take form.

Then urgency. If not the same, still kin to the fire that had burned in him all his life, he knew. The fire he'd fought, run from, been defeated by.

He tightened his grip on the railing. Below, at the crossroads, the semi stopped at the light and then lurched forward. Shifting into gear after gear it hur-tled up the highway, picking up speed till the cross-ing's light must have seemed a mere streak of red in the rearview mirror.

I should be in that truck, Frank thought. *Not here.* Not anywhere he'd be tempted to act on impulse. He had no right on earth to do what he was about to do now.

He turned the woman whose arms held him fast and drew her into his own embrace. Only one journey mattered now, if anything mattered at all. And that was the journey that Frank's mouth began as it moved to cover Kate's.

Her heartbeat thundered.

She'd meant to comfort him, that's all. Just a tender touch to share his pain. But the stroke of his mouth on hers brought an unexpected quickening, filling Kate like the first spring rain fills a parched arroyo and turns it into a raging river.

He parted her lips and deepened the kiss. Then the hard, hot taste of a hidden promise shot from his tongue to hers, stroking a single unspoken demand.

She would have met it willingly, but he pulled her body hard against his. Then as suddenly as he had initiated it, he broke the kiss. "You asked a question about my past," he said. "Have I answered it adequately?"

His voice was as bruising as his lips had been. He released her and Kate stepped back.

She reached for the steadying edge of the railing. "You said you weren't a criminal. I believe you."

"I said I hadn't broken any laws. I've done other things, though. Things I'm not proud of."

"You said you'd changed."

"I said I *hoped* I'd changed. I'm my father's son, Kate. I can't change that."

"An alcoholic—"

"Hardly." He laughed, the sound of it dry and bitter. "I don't drink. I never have."

The muted glow of the overhead porch light cast a dark shadow down one side of his face. On the other side, Kate read defiance.

"What is it then?"

He reached out again but his touch was gentle, stroking her shoulder where an arc of porch light fell over it. He traced a forefinger down the length of her arm, paused in the hollow at its bend, continued with exquisite slowness toward her wrist.

Kate closed her eyes, under his power as he caught her hand, raised it between them and brushed her curled fingers with a kiss. Then he pulled her closer, his warm breath searing her eyelids.

"Danger comes in unexpected forms."

Her eyes shot open. Her fingers ached with the pressure of his grasp.

"Do you see, *now?*" he asked her.

His eyes burned into hers. With fury? Passion? Lust? Kate couldn't be sure, but whatever it was, it was raw and wild. It drew her like a magnet.

"The men in my family could never be trusted," Frank said, "especially not with fragile women."

"*Fragile* women? Do you think I'd be living out here in the middle of nowhere if I couldn't take care of myself?"

A corner of his mouth crept toward a wry half smile. Anger flashed through Kate's body, sharp as a stroke of heat lightning. "You're making fun of me."

"No."

"What then?"

"I wanted to warn you. Perhaps it wasn't necessary."

"Fine. You've done that. Now, if you don't mind, I may not be fragile but I do need my sleep." She turned her back and jerked open the screen door.

* * *

The door slammed and Frank hit the path with a resolute stride. He would *not* look back. He would not *think* back. Not that he needed to. The taste of her mouth was still on his tongue, sweet and hot and smooth as racing suit satin.

It was going to be all he could manage to keep himself under control for the few days he'd agreed to stay at the crossing. Maybe he had changed and maybe he hadn't. He was damn well going to find out. But not at the expense of Kate Newton Prescott, or her son.

Still, that night he dreamed of her.

She was calling someone. Pretended anger laced her tone, a curious mix of the softness he'd seen that first time she'd served him coffee, and the fire she'd let loose when she'd torn her blouse, the fire that bloomed when she'd answered his kiss with a passion that nearly rivaled his own.

She was calling someone in the dream. Her son? No, it was not Bobby's voice that answered but his own. And that filled him with fear, not for himself, but for Kate. Because he was still a Vincenti, still filled with nameless anger, nameless passion, nameless need. . . .

It seemed just minutes later that he awoke to a knock on his door. Frank crushed the pillow and buried his head, but the banging came again.

"Up and at 'em, Mister Hotshot Fix-it man. It's almost dawn." A good-sized head poked through the open, screenless window. Frank groaned.

"B'golly, the man sleeps in the nude," Bo said. "We got somethin' in common after all. If you want stuff from Summit City, you better haul butt and open up. I got to leave early on account of an order."

Frank rolled out of bed, the sheet wrapped around him, and unlocked the motel room door.

Moments later Bo looked up from the list and took the watch Frank held out. "You *gotta* be kiddin'. Pawnshop ain't gonna give you but a couple hundred, maybe three at the most. Damn thing's worth four times that price. I'd buy it m'self if I had the bucks."

Frank pulled on jeans over navy-colored briefs. "I never cared for that watch," he said. "Take whatever they give you. Get as much of the stuff on the list as you can."

Bo studied the scrap of paper. "Them's long-legged jeans."

"I'm not the only tall man in Nevada."

"You sure you don't want to come along? Kate won't mind you takin' a break."

"I have to keep an eye on the stucco patches, keep them damp so they dry without cracks. Did you ask her about the paint?"

"She said it don't matter. I was thinkin' maybe pink."

Frank glanced up from pulling the cuff of his jeans down over the top of his boot.

"There's lots of pink stucco around," Bo insisted. "It's a popular color, 'specially down toward Tucson."

"Get a nice shade of beige and some dark brown glossy for the doors and the trim." Frank reached for his wallet and pulled out all but two of the fives. He thought of the credit cards lying useless on his bureau at home and tossed the wallet onto the bed. "Take this cash, you might need it."

"Kate gave me a check."

"Give it back to her after I'm gone."

Bo shoved the money into his pocket and pulled the watch over his wrist. He held it up to the light, admiring the glint of the gold. "How long you plannin' on staying, Frank?"

"I figure I'll finish in about four days. One thing more. That wood Bobby wants? Get fiberglass instead."

"Where the hell am I gonna find that?"

"Boat shop, auto body shop. Look around."

"I don't know nothin' about working with that stuff."

"You'll learn, Bo. You're a damn quick study."

"Yeah?"

Frank opened the door and headed outside.

The two men crossed the parking lot and parted at the Saguaro's back door. Bo heaved himself up into the cab of the pickup. Its engine coughed twice before it finally rolled over. The rusty blue truck lurched forward.

Frank stepped aside to avoid the dust. Bad timing, a dirty carburetor and God knows what else, he thought.

A few minutes later Frank was checking the job list when Kate came into the dish room. She hesitated, shifting the tub to one hip.

"There's a new brand of sausage for breakfast, and there'll be homemade vegetable soup for lunch," she said. She moved to the sink beside him, stacked dishes in a rack and lowered it into the sink.

"I'm not hungry now. Maybe I'll stop in—"

"You can't keep on skipping breakfast, surviving on a sandwich for lunch, then showing up when the dinner pot's nearly empty, Frank." She turned on the hot water, hard. "Our deal was room *and* board. If you'd rather have a salary—"

"Do you want me to stay?"

"We have an agreement."

"It included work inside the café. You've crossed those jobs off."

A slow rise of heat crept up her throat. She turned off the water.

"I still want the shelves put together. And the front screen door should stay on the list. They just don't need immediate attention, that's all. You can—"

"Hey, Mom, where's Frank?" Bobby crashed in through the back screen door, his sneakers untied, his book bag spilling papers.

"You're up early, kid."

Bobby grinned at Frank and shook disheveled hair out of his eyes.

"Could it be that you didn't quite finish your homework last night?" Kate asked. "That you're looking for help again?"

"Aw, Mom. I got my spelling done."

"And your math?"

Bobby shrugged and pulled a book out of his overstuffed bag. "I was reading this book..."

"*Wheels for Home Projects.* I know. I don't think it will pass book report muster with your teacher, Bobby."

"That's 'cause Miss White likes all those girls' books. Margaret Smith got an *A* on *Little Women,* and she didn't even do pictures."

Bobby's arms were full, so Frank bent down and Bobby dutifully pushed one sneaker forward to be tied, then the other.

"I got all but two problems done, Frank. I thought maybe over breakfast—" Bobby broke off and looked up at his mother.

"Okay. You have to eat. *Both* of you."

Frank pulled the laces snug, then Bobby bounded for the dish room doorway.

"You're good with shoelaces," Kate said to Frank.

"I've had lots of practice. My brother, Jesse . . ." A sudden tightening in his throat closed off the words. Memories of Jesse as a boy merged into thoughts of his funeral.

Kate touched his arm. "Go sit with Bobby. I'll bring you coffee."

He let her serve him. He kept wanting to get up, to tell *her* to sit. He'd never been waited on in his life, not by someone who knew him.

But then Bobby finished his cereal and opened his math book, and Frank lost himself in the present, doing something for this towheaded kid that he'd done too seldom for his brother, something with books, not cars. If he'd steered Jesse that way from the beginning . . .

Maybe helping Bobby made up for it. Maybe. And maybe it was risky.

Bobby left for school and the café filled, then emptied, then filled up again. Kate was too busy to mention the job list. Frank would disappear for a while outside, then just as she found herself looking for him he'd be back.

By the time Bo returned, Frank had the new dish shelves assembled. He helped the cook unload the truck, then Kate and the cook held the shelf system steady while Frank anchored it to the wall.

When they'd finished, Bo pulled a fold of bills from his coveralls pocket, along with a tattered list and a purple cardboard ticket. Kate recognized the well-known calling card from Pete's Pawn Palace in Summit City.

"Worse than I expected," Bo grumbled.

"Never mind," Frank said. He shoved the bills and receipt into his pocket, picked up the tool belt and headed for the café's front door.

"That guy sure is touchy," Bo muttered to Kate. "I done the best I could on his watch."

"I should have *made* him accept a salary."

"Now, Kate—"

"He obviously needs the job, Bo, and with spring cleaning we're lucky he came along when he did."

"Mattie says you're turning the café into a hospital camp again."

"We do the same chores every spring."

"You *are* kinda full of energy lately, ain't ya?"

"Don't say *ain't*, Bo. Bobby's picking it up."

Bo rocked back on his heels. "It's okay, Kate. I know the feelin'. Kinda miss the excitement of the old days myself sometimes."

Kate spun around. "Bo Thompson, biking nearly cost you Mattie. Neither one of us is going to get anywhere by looking back."

Bo sighed and scratched the back of his neck. "We sure as hell need *somethin'* to liven things up around here."

"Spring cleaning, that's what." Excitement was the last thing the crossing needed. She'd had enough of that with Charlie to last a lifetime, Kate thought.

She'd clean top to bottom, inside to out, sorting her thoughts as she did it, discarding whatever it was that had made her think, for even a minute, that she wanted another man in her life—wanted him so badly that she'd waited for that kiss without even knowing it from the moment Frank Vincenti had first swung out of Trav's truck and into her life.

But he continued to ignore her listed priorities.

All through the afternoon Frank worked at the jobs on the inside of the café. Oh, he kept his distance. Maybe he was trying to undo whatever it was he thought he had done last night; maybe he was trying to show her that the kiss really had been just a warning.

He finished fixing the short in the milk shake machine and went to work on the loose strip of metal edging on the counter. She held it taut while he hammered it back into place. Then he nailed down a loose floorboard behind the counter and remounted one of the sagging curtain brackets. She stood back and told him when it was level. He splinted a cracked table; she held the glued pieces while he wrapped the twine.

Customers wandered in and out. Kate moved back and forth from serving them to helping Frank, as though she'd been doing it for years, as though they were old friends who had never touched, never wondered what would happen if they did.

She was reaching to dust a far blade on the overhead ceiling fan when the ladder she was standing on swayed. Kate sucked in her breath.

Then, as suddenly as it had shifted, the ladder steadied. She looked down to see Frank anchoring it, one boot on the lower rung, two strong hands on the sides. His silver blue eyes held hers as steadily as he held the ladder.

Half a second more and she'd have been in his arms, Kate thought. Half a dozen steps down and she would be.

"Okay?" he asked, his voice husky.

She could only nod. He went back to the counter and the stool he'd been fixing, and Kate went back to dusting the fan, careful this time not to climb too high or reach too far. She was falling all right, but not from any ladder. She'd be lucky if she didn't break every bone in her body. If her heart had bones, she'd break them, too.

Should she take the list down and tell him she didn't need him any longer? Then he'd be gone with the first southbound trucker.

Or should she wait? See what happened? She was good at doing that. Then it would be his choice, not hers. His fault. Not hers. Even if she just kept going on as she was, living in the past as Ev said.

He worked on the screen door, shortening and reattaching the spring. He measured, cut and tacked heavy felt weather stripping into the jamb. Bobby came running from the bus and shot through the door as usual. The boy spun around to catch the door before it slammed, then stared in surprise as it closed with hardly a sound. Bobby whooped and stretched to give Frank a high five. Kate laughed and Frank grinned, bent down and matched his large hand against her son's smaller one.

Kate's laughter went inward then, slow and deep as a kettle covered over and switched to simmer.

Then a customer came through the door, and it swung closed quietly behind him. She'd endured three years of that slamming door, Kate thought. Maybe she'd endured a lot of other things needlessly, too.

Chapter Four

Bo came in at quarter to four. He banged around in the dish room for half an hour, then emerged with a hefty-sized baking pan poised on his shoulder.

"Meat loaf," he muttered as he shoved the pan into the oven. "Mashed potatoes on the side."

"Save some?" Frank said.

"Yeah, maybe. If you're not too late."

Frank slung the tool belt over his shoulder and started for the door.

"Truck's actin' funny," Bo called after him.

Frank stopped, his hand on the screen door. He knew what was coming.

"You got time to take a look under the hood?"

The job was for a handyman, not a mechanic, he wanted to say. If he picked up one wrench, there would soon be others.

"Frank can fix anything, I bet," Bobby said.

"I pulled 'er into a bay. She's leakin' oil bad." Bo set the timer he'd been winding on the shelf above the oven.

Frank searched for something to say, some way to explain his reluctance to have anything to do with trucks, cars, anything with an engine and wheels. Kate's eyes caught his and softened.

"You've worked a long day," she said. "The truck can wait till tomorrow."

But they needed the old truck. They needed his skills. Why wait till after California to try to figure out how much of the old life he wanted to hang on to?

"I'll take a look," he said, and went out the door before he had to say more.

But another car had pulled into the adjoining bay alongside the old pickup. The blue-and-white Nevada State Patrol cruiser coughed and shuddered to a stop.

Frank took his time crossing the street.

Bobby's teacher leaned against the rear bumper of the cruiser. Something about her was different, maybe her hairstyle or the dark glasses. The hood of the cruiser was up. All Frank could see of MacMillan were polished black boots, two stout trousered legs and the gun belt.

The woman shot him a smile as sultry as any he'd ever seen at the racetrack. "Bo claims you worked a miracle on that swamp cooler motor," she whispered. "When we passed the garage, I told Mac you must be working on the truck. You could look at the patrol car, too, I suggested."

"I'm not a mechanic," Frank said abruptly.

MacMillan's head shot up, banging hard on the open hood. A stream of curse words exploded. The teacher's face turned crimson.

"I told Ev, most likely you'd know as much about cars as she does," Mac sputtered, adjusting his hat.

"I didn't say I don't know cars," Frank answered evenly.

Mac looked at him, hard. "So take a look."

A thin sheet of oil still smoked where it hit the hot metal of the block. Frank touched a spot, rubbed the residue between two fingers and reached for a rag.

"It can't be anything major," Mac said. "I just had her in for service, and the highway patrol's maintenance shop is top-notch."

"What did they do?"

The trooper shrugged. "The usual stuff. Rotate the tires, check the belts, change the oil...you think maybe the filter worked loose or something? There's a hell of a lot of oil on the engine."

"Why don't you and the lady go across the street and get dinner? I should have an answer by the time you're finished."

Mac's eyes narrowed. Frank knew what the man was thinking. *Where's the drifter who wants nothing to do with cops?*

Not all policemen. Just one, a long time ago in another place. And his brother had thrown the first punch.

The Saguaro's screen door swung open and Mac came in, followed by Ev. "We're going to the movies," she said. "Mac's got tickets for a sneak preview, that new documentary. If it weren't a school night, I'd invite Bobby.''

MacMillan colored and turned away to hang his hat on the peg behind the door. When he saw the grease spot across the crown, he groaned and pulled out his handkerchief.

Ev snatched the hat. "Don't *wipe* it, silly, you'll smear the stain. Kate, do you have some extra baking soda?''

Mac slumped down on a stool, looking, Kate thought, like a stray tomcat who'd just been hauled to a child's tea party. He pulled out the menu he knew by heart and hunched over it.

"Order me something light,'' she called back to the trooper. Mac didn't look up.

In the dish room Ev dusted the stain, brushed off the soda, then dusted it again. The oil began to fade.

"I'm glad it *is* a school night, and happy you're letting Mac take you out,'' Kate said.

Ev gave a quick laugh. "It's not exactly a date. I invited him and offered to pay if he'd go in early and pick up the tickets.''

"Bobby said he dropped you at school this morning.''

"He was giving a talk on pedestrian safety, and since we were going to the movies—''

"Ev, this is the nineties. You don't need an excuse to go after a man. It's not like it was when we were kids.''

The teacher spun around so quickly a cloud of soda jumped from the box and rose in the air between them. "You've got *that* right. Back then we waited. Most of us did, anyway.''

Kate was silent, enduring Ev's unspoken accusation. She took the box of soda, folded down the top and set it on the shelf above the sink.

Ev brushed Mac's hat as though determined to wear that grease stain right through the felt. "*Some* of us, as I recall, were pretty darn aggressive even back then."

Maybe if she tried again, Ev would give her a chance to explain, Kate thought. She hadn't even known about Nonnie Prescott's silly little scheme, inviting Ev to go out on that blind date with her cousin from California, then getting mad at some little slight and taking Kate instead. It was all so ironic. Charlie's carefree nature had touched some latent wild streak, and Kate had responded. But she'd have given anything to have fallen in love with a local boy. Ev, on the other hand, had wanted to get away from the crossing. Charlie could have been her ticket.

"Let's go on out and see what Mac's ordered you for dinner," Kate said, touching Ev's hand to still it.

Ev's eyes met hers and the accusing frown eased into a wistful one. "He probably didn't get me anything. If he did, he'll ask me to pay."

"I've got strawberry pie for dessert and you're not going to pay for that—it's on the house."

"Your strawberry pie is Bobby's favorite," Ev said. A quick, bright smile flashed across the teacher's face, lighting her eyes and smoothing the lines around her mouth.

You're so pretty when you smile, Ev. Kate wanted to say it out loud, but the teacher turned quickly and headed for the door.

Mac had poured coffee for Ev, as well as for himself. And he'd ordered her a big chef's salad. Maybe there was hope for the man after all.

Mac tipped back his hat, then hung his thumbs in his belt. "That's *all* it was? A bum gasket? Give me a receipt. I'll see that you're reimbursed."

"No problem," Frank said. "I found the gasket in the back along with a case of oil. Nothing has prices, no books to speak of—"

"Old man Newton ran everything by the seat of his pants, especially near the end. You plan on doing the same?" The trooper rocked back on his heels and chewed his toothpick, his squinty eyes leveled on Frank. "Hell of an opportunity right here under your nose. Tools, parts, a sturdy building. Last I heard the lifts were on the blink, but a *good mechanic* could take care of that."

"He's not a mechanic," Ev said. She shot Frank a smile. "I sure wish you'd take a look at my old car, though. I like to look after things *before* they break down."

The trooper swung open the cruiser's passenger door. "The guy said he doesn't work on cars, Evelyn. If you want to make that movie, we'd better get going."

Mac slammed her door, went around to his own side, got in and slammed his own door.

"He's *so* possessive," Ev whispered, leaning out the window. She handed Frank a crumpled sheet of notebook paper. "Give this to Kate. She'll know what it's about."

Frank glanced at the sketched designs that decorated the scattered math problems. All of the answers were accurate. Had the teacher noticed?

Mac gunned the engine and Frank stepped aside as the car lurched out of the garage, paused on the street and then shot forward. At the healthy hum of the engine, Frank smiled. He was glad he'd gone ahead and made those extra adjustments.

"You change your mind about comin' in for supper, or are you back to feelin' contrary again?" Bo balanced the tray on one big hand, his other hand hooked in a six-pack of beer.

The smell of oregano and hot mashed potatoes brought Frank out from under the truck.

"Time goes fast when you're havin' fun, huh?" Bo nodded at the big clock over the office doorway.

Nine o'clock? *Damn.* He'd missed dinner, a chance to see Kate.

In the office Bo opened two beers, passed one across the desk, then lowered his heavy frame into the old swivel chair and propped up his feet. "You get the blue clunker purrin' again? Locate her problem?"

"Which one? That engine is stuck together with wire and chewing gum."

Bo chuckled. "They're doing the job, ain't...*aren't* they?"

Frank grinned and took a forkful of creamy mashed potatoes.

Bo peeled open the foil pouch with four of Kate's biscuits, took one himself and shoved the rest toward Frank. "I've kept the old buggy running," he said between bites. "Didn't have no choice."

"You're a good mechanic. How come you've kept it such a secret?"

The big man squinted across the desk. "Supposin' I ask *you* the very same question?"

Frank broke a biscuit. "It's been a long time since I've worked on a car myself."

"You got others who do it for you?"

"I . . . took over my father's business when he died twelve years ago. I've managed a team of mechanics and other personnel off and on since then."

"'Managed,' as in 'used to,' or are you still runnin' the show?"

"That part of my life is over. I'd just as soon forget it." Frank eyed the beer, then carried a chipped coffee mug to the sink, filled it with water and drained it with one swallow. He filled the mug again and sat down.

Bo leaned forward, his massive forearms crossed on the edge of the desk. "Your brother died, Kate said. He got killed, maybe in a car you worked on? You don't want nothin' to do with engines no more?"

"It's a little more complicated, but yes, that's about the way it happened."

Bo leaned back, satisfied. "Guess I know an engine man when I see one," he said. "Take that bike out back. She was a right nice machine before I slid her under a slow-movin' semi. Thank God I wasn't carrying Mattie."

The cook stood up and raised the back of his shirt. A crisscross pattern of angry scars covered his torso. It was amazing what asphalt could do the body, Frank thought, even through a biker's leather jacket. Asphalt and fire. If Jesse had been wearing the fireproof racing suit...if *he'd* made sure his younger brother—

"A man loses his taste for the road and all that goes along with it," Bo said. "Maybe he loses a hell of a lot more, like his nerve."

Frank's laugh was short and cynical. "It's a choice, Bo, nothing more."

Frank stood and strode to the doorway leading into the bays. He leaned against the jamb. Light from an overhead bulb swayed in the evening breeze. Shadows danced and for a moment he thought of another garage, other cars.

So quit. Leave the driving to Jesse. He's got what it takes. You don't.

"We ought to get the lift back in service," Bo said, coming up behind him.

Frank moved on into the garage and kicked the dolly into place, then stretched out on it. He pulled his way under the truck and switched on the swag light. *We don't need the lift,* Frank thought. He wouldn't be working on any more cars. Bo was right. He'd lost his taste for it, maybe more.

Bo hung around for an hour, passing him tools and trading stories, mostly about cheap tricks that could keep a car or a motorbike on the road forever, though not always successfully, they'd agreed. Bo told about the time he'd pushed a motorcycle halfway to Tucson, and Frank let it slip that he'd lost more races than he'd won when he was a kid because the car he'd been driving had died on the track.

"NASCAR?" Bo asked.

"Midgets and sprints. I never had a taste for stock car racing, even before I quit driving."

Bo didn't press, though he'd probably already guessed. Sprints and midgets led straight to the Indy circuit—everybody's dream, his, then Jesse's, from the time they'd been kids.

But not anymore.

Bo had gone out to work on his bike and try the adjustment they'd discussed. Frank worked a while longer then tightened the last of the bolts and switched off the swag light. He rested for a moment on the dolly. He closed his eyes.

The smells were the same. Almost. He'd kept his shop on Gasoline Alley cleaner, and each member of his team had been required to do the same. He could see them now in their crisp work coveralls, royal blue pinstripes on gray cotton twill, the silver-and-blue Team Vincenti falcon logo on each breast pocket.

And he could see the car.

The wreckage sat on blocks at the rear of the shop. He'd done his best not to look at it when he'd gone to the shop to deliver the keys to his lawyer.

Sell out. Make it quick.

Then he'd gone to the hospital. He'd held his brother's bandaged hand—

"Frank?"

Her voice was a quiet benediction, closing off the past. He rolled the dolly out and rose.

"It's late, I...we wondered...Frank, you look *exhausted.*"

Bobby passed him a steaming mug. "It's hot coffee, Frank. Bet you could use it."

He took the cup, smearing it with grease from his grimy touch. He chuckled with an edge of bitterness.

"My father always told me, 'Stay out of the pits if you want clean hands.'"

Bobby laughed. "The pits?"

"A term for the lanes on the inside edge of a race-track, kid, a place where cars are refueled and serviced."

It was Kate's turn to laugh. "Or a term for a broken-down grease pit of a garage somewhere in the middle of nowhere?"

His eyes laughed with her, then grew serious. He tapped the cup on a fender. "This truck will purr like a kitten tomorrow night when you take it down the highway for your meeting with Bobby's teacher."

"Bo calls it the old blue bomb," Bobby said. "I guess he thinks it's going to explode."

"No way, kid. This truck is going to take you to school when you miss the bus or your teacher's ride, and haul groceries for Bo for the next six months, maybe longer. This vehicle is going to be safe and useful. That pleases me more than I ever would have thought."

"It pleases me, too," Kate said. A wash of pink lit her cheeks. She bent her head briefly, then looked up, her green eyes bright as starlight.

"It's the crossing, Frank. It makes even simple things pleasurable."

No, it's you, he wanted to say. But Bobby was there. And he had no words, really. For her, for the place, about himself. Especially for her.

She stepped back abruptly, nearly upsetting the coffee cup perched on the fender of the car. She caught it just before it slid to the floor. Grease smeared her hands, too.

"Pop always said, 'Dirty hands, warm heart.' Of course, it's really, 'Cold hands, warm heart.'"

She stood there looking up at him, a blush trailing all the way down her throat, rosy against the pure white of her blouse. He cursed the grime on his hands that kept him from touching her, the dirty coveralls he'd found in the back of the garage, the grit in his eyes. God, how he wanted to hold her, wanted it so much it crossed his mind that it was good that the boy was there.

"We'd better get back," she said. "It's way past Bobby's bedtime."

"I'll walk you up the hill."

"No," she said gently. "Go to bed. Get some rest."

She swept by him then, leaving a trace of something that smelled like flowers. Bobby lingered, then followed when his mother called.

Frank switched out the light and locked the garage, then headed across the road toward the string of motel rooms beyond the café.

At his door, he paused and looked up the hill. The lamp on her porch was out, but in the soft drift of light from a rising moon he thought he saw a figure at the railing.

Last night came back to him then. The touch of Kate's hand on his chest, the wildflower scent that rose from her hair when he'd turned to hold her, the free and easy way she'd moved into his arms and welcomed his kiss. Then he'd lost control and ruined it all.

But he wanted another chance. Whatever else he'd have to give up, whatever else was waiting for him at the end of his journey, Frank wanted this woman in his arms.

In his bed.

The knowing shot through him, burned hot as racing fuel in his chest, churned in his gut. He wanted her, and he didn't want to wait. *Like Jesse,* he thought, who'd been so damn eager to get into the car he hadn't even bothered with the fireproof suit.

If he pushed too hard he'd risk losing Kate, the way he'd lost everything else. And more. He'd risk damaging the boy. It was best to keep his distance. From them both.

The full moon slid behind a cloud. The figure on the porch dissolved. It had been just a shadow, Frank thought, like most of his other dreams. Life was just a series of choices, like he'd told Bo. And he'd made so many wrong ones.

Frank was in the garage office that afternoon, mixing the paint for the motel's adobe walls, when Bobby came in. The boy tossed a booklet onto the desk, threw himself into the old swivel chair and glowered.

Frank stirred the paint. Bobby swiveled. The more the chair creaked, the faster he spun. Finally Frank put down the paddle and picked up the *All-American Soap Box Derby* rule book.

"I have to use official wheels."

"That gives you a problem?"

"I thought I'd just use the wheels off Grandpop's old lawn mower. They're in great shape. Bo helped me take 'em off. I've been cleaning them up. That's one of the rules. You have to do the work yourself."

"And another rule is that you have to use regulation wheels."

Bobby kicked the desk and spun the chair again. Frank dipped a paintbrush into a bucket of thinner and worked it back and forth. Jesse had been just as stubborn, as stiff and unbending as the old brush.

"I don't see *why* I have to use their wheels."

"It keeps the race safe, and fair."

Bobby stopped swiveling the chair. "I wouldn't want to win except by being fair."

Frank's hand stilled. His eyes met the boy's. "That's *good,*" he said gently.

"There's still a problem, though. The wheels cost fifteen dollars apiece. I need four. That's sixty dollars—"

"Good math. It does come in handy."

Bobby grinned sheepishly. "Still, I've only got twenty-two dollars and twelve cents left, and I don't get allowance till the end of the month."

I'll give you the money, kid. No, he'd done that too often with Jesse. He'd come to see it as part of the problem.

"I could help you paint."

"You've got school."

"I could tell Mom I'm sick, then get well by afternoon."

"Being honest is kin to being fair, kid."

"Yeah, well . . ."

Frank passed him the rule book and Bobby sighed and shuffled toward the door.

Frank picked up the paintbrush. Then he put it down again. "Tomorrow's Saturday."

Bobby turned back. "I could get up real early. Even before sunup."

"Eight o'clock's fine. After breakfast. Don't be late. And ask your mother."

Bobby hesitated. "I don't know. How about if I just tell her I want to help you out 'cause I want to earn extra money?"

Frank raised an eyebrow.

"It wouldn't be a lie."

"It wouldn't be the whole truth, either."

"She's going to get mad. I told her about the derby this morning. I was going to show her my car design, but she got real quiet the way she always does when she's going to say I'm too small or too young or too *something.*"

"*Are* you too—"

"Just because I'm short for nine years old doesn't mean I can't do anything the other guys can. I told Mom that, too. I don't think it mattered, but she's going to look at the rule book, at least. So can I help, Frank?"

"You're going to be late for school, kid."

"*Please?*"

It had been a long time since anyone had asked him for anything, Frank thought. Jesse made demands. Or went behind his back. Maybe it had been his fault. Maybe he'd been too strict. Or not strict enough.

"If your mother has chores, get them done first. Then come and see me."

"All *right!*"

The boy was out the door in a second. He barely stopped to look both ways before darting across the road to the café. He'd have to speak to the kid about that, Frank thought.

So much for keeping his distance.

It had been a long day and a busy evening at the restaurant, and Kate was wishing that the parent-teacher conference would end. At breakfast, she'd had that argument with Bobby about the derby race, then Mattie's sick headache had meant she'd had to work lunch alone. And tomorrow would be worse. The festival down the road would bring busloads of tourists. She wouldn't even get a chance to talk to Frank.

Kate sat at the small school desk, feeling like a cranky third grader. "Ev, I don't see the problem. Bobby's doing fine on his tests."

"His homework is downright sloppy."

To meet Ev's eyes she'd have to look up, so Kate looked down at her hands, clasped loosely in her lap. Her palms were damp. *Ridiculous*. Kate chuckled to herself.

"It's *no* laughing matter," Ev said sternly. She shook out the wrinkled paper and slid it into a crisp manila folder, a stamped red star on its tab. Kate wondered what the red star stood for.

Suddenly she didn't care. "I've got to get back to the Saguaro. I told Bo I'd do the pies."

Ev took forever working the rubber band to the exact middle of the folder. Then she leaned back and pursed thin lips. "I've saved this till the end of our talk, Kate. I wanted to see how you'd take the news that Bobby's not working up to his potential. As I suspected, you're not concerned at all."

"That's not true. I'm as concerned as any parent, but he's just a child, Ev."

"You don't know what you have here. Bobby is special. The results of that new California test came back yesterday. You remember the information packet that the school sent home?"

Kate wanted to fib. She'd skimmed the report briefly, then filed it away. She'd been so busy—

"Bobby scored exceptionally high. He's a very bright little boy, Kate. As his only parent, you have a special responsibility." Ev opened her drawer and took out a pamphlet.

The sleek brochure, titled *The Gifted Child,* pictured an astronaut, a scientist and a physician. Kate's heart swelled with pride. Then Ev shoved a second brochure across the table.

Desert Sands Boarding School.

She met Ev's accusing gaze with a level one of her own. "I've always known about Bobby's intelligence, Ev, but I want him to have a normal childhood."

"A *normal* childhood? You call life at the crossing *normal?* Even when we were growing up there was nothing to do and nowhere to go. That's why everyone moved away." Ev tapped her fingers on the banded folder. "I can tell what day of the week these assignments were done just by the food that's been spilled on them. It's no wonder Bobby's homework is sloppy. How any child can be expected to work in a *restaurant—*"

Kate stood up so quickly the boarding school brochure flew off the teacher's desk and floated to the floor. Kate snatched it up. "Bobby has his own room at home, his own desk and two sets of encyclopedias, both of which he's working on reading from *A* to *Z*. He has his dog and his clubhouse and friends who spend the weekend. And he does his homework over dinner every night of the week at the Saguaro because that's where he wants to be.''

Kate shoved the brochures into her purse and slung the strap over her shoulder. At the door she turned back. ''Ev, maybe Bobby does need more stimulation, but there's no reason he can't get that at the crossing. There are lots of things to do.''

''Like building that soap box derby car? You know as well as I do that Bobby shouldn't waste his time on things like that.''

Tell that to your new principal, Kate almost said. But she clamped her mouth shut. She would not give Ev the satisfaction of knowing that Bobby had mentioned the race car only just that morning.

She pushed open the classroom door and strode down the hall, past the row of empty lockers, past the bulletin board with its construction paper butterflies, past the principal's office. She could stop and talk to the principal about the race. She'd promised Bobby she'd at least do that. Maybe she'd even go ahead and sign the permission form right then.

But if she faced Mr. Peterson now, her anger would show, and the last thing Kate wanted to do was explain why she was furious.

It wasn't true. Newton's Crossing had never been a place where nothing happened. Where else could you see so deeply, so often, with so little surface light, into the starlit night sky? Bobby knew every major constellation. She'd taught them to him just as Pop had taught her.

And he knew the wildlife and the flowers and that there were six varieties of spiders—*arachnids,* he delighted in calling them—underneath the flagstone downspout. He'd met people from every state in the union and seven foreign countries. He could say hello in eight languages, for heaven's sake.

Kate climbed into the truck and slammed the door. She fumbled for her keys, her eyes stinging as she thought of Bobby, small and lonely, trudging off to some live-in school. He would be miserable.

She would be miserable.

And one less student, or just a few more, might mean they'd close the school down for good. The bus ride would stretch to over an hour each way for most of the kids. They'd drop out as soon as they could, move away, maybe never come back. It was a cycle she'd seen repeated all her life. Now Ev was suggesting...

Kate took a breath of warm, dry air to clear her head. Even if there was some grain of truth to Ev's words, boarding school was not the solution.

She shoved the gearshift into position and backed up, wheels spinning in the loose desert gravel, and bumped down the road toward the highway. The library in Summit City was open late on Fridays. If she hurried, she'd have time to swing by. She'd take out everything they had on the subject of siphons, Bobby's latest interest, and anything new on spiders. Maybe he'd forget about the car.

Little boys. Little cars. *Rock Top Mountain.* The soap box derby had always been there, on the easy slope of the southern approach. Not the side that looked north, up across the state line toward Edwards Air Force Base in California, not the steep, sheer face with its deep vee cleft just wide enough for a jet to slip through. *Big boys, big planes they treated like toys.*

Kate stepped on the gas and the old truck shot forward with unexpected tenacity. The speedometer inched up toward fifty. Odd, she thought. The needle had not gone higher than forty-five in years. She thought of Frank and smiled.

Bo rocked back and rubbed his stomach, full from the late-night stewed chicken supper he'd shared at the garage with Frank. He watched with the protective eyes of an overeager father as Frank walked around the bike.

"Them's virgin tires, front and rear. Cost me like hell, but worth every penny."

"New clutch?"

"Built it myself. No sense havin' a good runnin' motor if you smoke out the clutch."

Bo squatted and opened a new red toolbox, then took out a series of wrenches, each one shinier than the last.

"Nice ratchet," Frank commented.

"Don't do no good to build the best 'less you can take care of it right. Ain't no tight spot that baby can't reach. You got 'em at your place?"

"It's not my place anymore."

"Oh, yeah, you're sellin'. Got any takers?"

"Patrick, Galles, Penske . . . they'd have paid for a thirty-second look under the chassis last year. I guess they'll go for the whole operation now."

Bo let out a low whistle. "Them's high-powered racing teams. You part of the big league, Frank?"

"I had a foot in the door."

Sudden understanding swept Bo's heavy face. "Your brother, the one who died, his name was Jesse, wasn't it? You got that burn when you pulled him out."

"Not fast enough."

"I read about it. They said he took the car out without permission, that it hadn't been cleared."

"The press said a lot of things. I was responsible. It was my car, he was my brother. But I'm free of racing now."

"Free? Hey, it's bikers, engine gurus, the fools that climb into those cars you build—we're the ones who are really free. We don't give a thought to tomorrow, and yesterday's just a mirage. *Freedom*—that's what it's all about." Bo stroked the tattered seat of his bike.

"Freedom from what?"

"Ain't no sense lookin' back to see. If you get a good look at what's chasin' you, you might just up and quit running. Ever wonder what *that* would be like?"

Frank didn't answer. He was staring out through the open garage door, up the hill behind the darkened café, up toward the house and the light on the porch.

"Course maybe it'd be like it is now and then when Mattie ain't feelin' so ornery. Quiet, peaceful, full." Bo was silent a minute, then he tossed the wrench onto the tarp and reached for another. "But I ain't no good when it comes time to stand and deliver. Got two missin' teeth and a twice-broke nose to prove that. It's best to keep on movin', and lately I been feelin' the urge.'' He bent over the cycle to make an adjustment.

A breeze blew in through the open doorway, and on it came a thread of laughter. Up on the hill a lone figure waved and headed down the path. Mattie. Bobby ran down off the porch, gave her a hug, then ran back to where his mother held the open screen door.

Two women, one boy. Three reasons for two men to let go of the past, plan for the future, quit running. Bo had an inkling of what it would cost. Frank knew for sure.

He'd thought about it all afternoon, with every stroke of the brush on the rough stucco walls.

Kate had stopped on the way to her meeting, to badger him for working so hard. He'd waved a brush at the clogged parking lot and given her some of the same.

He could still see her eyes, see the way they'd filled up with laughter, like clear green water tripping over pebbles in a spring-fed Indiana brook.

She'd tipped her nose, hands on hips, and swung her braid over her shoulder. "You can't think unless you're working on some mindless task," she'd told him. "Neither can I. You paint. I clean. I'm always that way, at least in the spring."

"*Just* in the spring?"

She'd looked away, her gaze distant. He stepped close, touched her arm. The green eyes swung back and widened.

She looked up at him then. Unflinchingly. With absolute trust.

He wanted to withdraw his question, shake his head, shake *her*. He'd tightened his hold on her arm.

"Other times, too," she said quickly. "It's just that in the spring it's a little harder to control."

"I shouldn't have asked."

"Why not? I can trust you with my secret. I'm an *excellent* judge of character."

You're mistaken this time, he'd wanted to say. *You don't know what you're getting into.* He'd wanted to warn her again.

But she laughed, bubbling over with that music she made when she did it. It played his heart like a violin, till he had to sip the sound of it from her lips like new May wine.

He'd kissed her then, just a light brush of his lips to hers. And she kissed him back, then laughed and pulled away, hurrying off to keep her appointment.

It wasn't just him she trusted, he knew. Kate was a believer. In things, in people, in life. She could teach him that if he stayed long enough. And if he stayed—

"You got any more brilliant ideas about how to get the lead outa this engine?"

Frank turned from the doorway, back to Bo and the bike. Squatting, he examined the bike's crumpled front fender, the metal twice as heavy as it needed to be. Before he'd checked the size of the bolts, Bo was slapping a wrench in his hand.

They worked late on the bike, trading stories and jokes then falling into companionable silence. A few times they argued and Frank acquiesced. Bo was the bike expert. No amount of general engine training could compare to his knowledge of every nut, bolt, bracket and wire on the machine he called his "second love."

Bone tired, Frank finally rose and headed out, leaving Bo still at work on the bike.

He stumbled into his room, washed up, then fell into bed, his face to the pillow that smelled, he thought briefly, the same as Kate's hair.

He thought of her then. Imagined her bending over him, her soft braid sweeping his face. Warmth moved through his body, became an elusive memory, then finally a dream.

Kate. Walking toward him, barefoot in a meadow of green clover. A simple cotton dress. A picnic spread on the grass. A red-checked cloth. Strawberries. Nothing more to eat, but he wasn't hungry. Cool water. Cool kisses. Then warm ones. Her body, naked. The rise of her breasts, hard nipples at his mouth.

Kate!

He woke once to the sound of a hushed argument—Bo's low grumble, Mattie's lighter protest—then again later to the rumble of the motorcycle. The new ignition setting must have done the trick. He tossed for a moment and then reached again for the dream.

Chapter Five

"Fine night Frank picked to overhaul the cooler's motor again," Mattie grumbled.

Kate tugged at her scoop-neck pink T-shirt till it bloused more modestly. "I thought it was going to be cool. We're usually closed by now on Saturday nights anyway."

"You also thought we were done with tourists. I haven't seen this many buses since Bo and I left Vegas."

"It's nearly eight, it's got to end soon."

Bo stuck his head in the dish room doorway. "Could you ladies *kindly* get with it? We've got more folks comin' in and they look hungry."

It had taken all of them working at a constant pace to keep the Friday and Saturday customers happy.

Then an overcast sky had trapped the heat and made matters worse.

"I can't believe that festival up the road ran out of food again," Mattie said.

"*I* can't believe I forgot that they'd asked me to manage a booth." Kate shook her head ruefully.

"You've had your mind on something—or *somebody*—else all week."

Kate blushed and ducked into the ice bin to hide it. "The darn entry fee was too high anyway." She scooped out a pitcher full of cubes and passed it to Mattie, took another empty pitcher and bent down again. Her voice echoed into the bin.

"I'll tell you another thing, Mattie. One of these years, if we start planning early enough, we could have our own festival right here in Newton's Crossing. We could get Summit City Federal to rent us the old hardware store for a weekend and send out letters to local craftsmen—"

"Yeah, sure."

"And fit the church with standing dividers for a good-size art exhibit. The kids could even do face painting in Ev's mother's old beauty salon."

"What about the roulette wheel in the basement of the jail? Mac's sure suggested we use *that* often enough."

Kate ducked out of the ice bin. "I'll never vote for gambling at the crossing, and you'd better not, ei-ther, Mattie Thompson." She grabbed a pitcher and leaned in again for more ice. "Why bring the crossing back to life if all we have to sustain it is gambling?" she yelled.

"Maybe they'd play all night and stay over for church on Sundays," Mattie yelled back. "Course, then you'd have to keep the Saguaro open for brunch, and I sure as hell am *not* going to work on Sundays."

"I wouldn't mind, and church would be nice. We could open at noon...." She'd ducked out of the bin but Mattie was gone. Frank stood in her place.

"Church *would* be nice," he said. "I haven't been in years." He tossed his sweat-soaked shirt on an empty box and took the pitcher of ice Kate was holding, turned and filled it with water, then lifted it and drank from the side.

A rivulet of water slid down the side of his face, dripped off his jaw to a sun-bronzed shoulder, then disappeared into the shiny black mat of hair on his chest. Kate's throat pricked, suddenly hot and dry. She moistened her lips. Frank lowered the pitcher and met her eyes.

"I'm sorry I asked you to rebuild that motor tonight," Kate said. "It's too hot...." His eyes had slipped to her mouth. Now they traveled down her body. She tugged at her clinging cotton T-shirt.

He tipped the pitcher and drank again. The bird on his shoulder seemed to spread its wings and stir the air.

He finished drinking and wiped his mouth with the back of his hand. She'd reached up to tighten her braid, loose from a long day of working and the heat. His eyes traced the twisting motion of her fingers.

"You have beautiful hair."

Her hand stilled. The slow, soft thrumming that she hadn't been able to control all week began again at the base of her belly.

He ran a hand through his own dark hair. Damp and unruly, it tangled in his fingers. She thought of the way it had curled around her fingers that night on the porch.

"You need a haircut," Kate heard herself say. "I could do it Sunday. Tomorrow. Up at the house after dinner."

She'd rehearsed the invitation all afternoon. Now it had just come out, crazy, disordered. She'd try again. "I was wondering if you'd like to join me...*us*. Bobby, Mattie, Bo. On Sundays the Saguaro's closed. We have a sort of family tradition. Dinner at three. It's my turn to cook. Will you come?"

What was it she'd told Ev? *It's okay to go after a man.* But it wasn't okay, Kate thought. Not if he refused.

"Mom! The horses are here."

Kate spun around. Bobby wore the old oversize pair of chaps they'd found at the secondhand store in Summit City. She'd promised. Now she'd have to back down again.

"Bobby, the café's crazy tonight. I had to call Mattie in. And you must be exhausted after working all day with Frank."

"I'm okay, Mom, and you don't have to go with me. I can handle Brandy real good by myself. You said so yourself the last time we rode."

"But Bobby—"

"Come on, Mom. I'm old enough. I've been riding since I was *four!*"

But never on the night trail alone. If something happened to him out on the desert, if he were thrown and knocked unconscious, bitten by a snake...

"Bobby, let's see if the man can bring the horses around next weekend. Let's ask—"

"Oh, *Mom.*" Bobby punched a cloth bag of rice and a few grains escaped through a tear. "I'm not a baby anymore, Mom, *damn it* anyway."

"Cursing won't prove you're grown-up, young man."

Bobby shoved a sneaker through the scattered rice. "I'm sorry, Mom." Then his chin shot up. "I guess *you* wouldn't want to go riding tonight, would you, Frank?"

Slowly, as though buying time, Frank poured the water and ice down the sink. He set the pitcher on the dish drain. "I used to ride with...my brother, but that was a long time ago." He reached for his shirt and began to pull it on.

Bobby's eyes widened. "Did you have your own horse? Did you ride all the time?"

Frank laughed gently. "My father's people had a farm in Indiana. I rode Relentless when I could catch him. He didn't belong to me or anybody else."

"Please, Mom, can Frank come with me?"

"Bobby, he's worked all day."

"I'm not tired." Frank bent over the faucet to splash water on his face.

"The cloud cover's hiding the moonlight, but the trail is marked with fluorescent paint. Bobby knows the way." Kate raised her voice over the sound of the water. "I'd be very grateful."

Frank turned, his face dripping water, inches from her own. "You don't need to be grateful," he said.

His voice swept over her, an imagined caress that drew her as strongly as a real one. She took a step back and bumped a pile of dishes.

"Let's go!" Bobby said.

"Be back by ten-thirty or you'll miss the late movie with Mattie," Kate said.

"Sure, Mom." Bobby had stuffed an apple in one pocket and was trying to work a raw carrot into the other. "It's a good thing you're used to strong-minded horses," he said to Frank. "Mom always asks for Blaze 'cause he's the wildest one they've got."

Frank lifted an eyebrow. A corner of his mouth followed suit. Kate colored and bent down to scoop up the scattered rice.

She didn't look up till the door had swung closed behind them and the voices outside had faded.

Her son had been drawn to Frank from the day he'd arrived, Kate knew. A dozen times or more she'd missed Bobby, only to find him out back painting with Frank, or in the garage, even once up on the roof. Her heart had stopped that time, till she'd seen Frank stand up and put a steadying hand on the boy's shoulder. Then Bobby had glanced up with the same adoring look that he'd worn just now, and Kate had felt another, less definite fear. How would her son feel when Frank decided it was time to go?

How would *she* feel?

Kate shook off the thought, grabbed a roll of silver duct tape and tore off a piece. She pressed it over the tear in the big bag of rice, then scooped up the few remaining grains.

The pearllike drops nestled in her hand. She and Bobby had so much love between them. Couldn't they afford to share a few grains and come away undiminished? Wasn't that what life at the crossing was all about, nurturing those who happened along, sending them on their way full of good hot food and a touch of human kindness? Kate smiled to herself. It wasn't just kindness that had been on her mind all week.

She'd been waiting for someone like Frank since long before he'd swung out of Trav's truck and into her life. She'd been waiting all winter, maybe waiting since Charlie had died. No, long before that. Waiting for a man she could trust.

She'd trusted Charlie, once, and that had ended badly. Where would this end? Did it have to end?

Almost an hour to the minute after Bobby and Frank had ridden out, the café's business dropped off. So did the temperature. There wasn't any need to switch on the cooler. As she stood at the Saguaro's front door watching Mattie and Bo cross the street to the trailer, Kate thought she heard the rumble of thunder.

But there had been no lightning, and a moment later a noisy semi pulled up at the gas pumps across the street.

The trucker paid and headed on down the road, and Kate locked the pumps and turned the café's sign to closed. She cleared the register, dropped the day's receipts into the small safe under the counter and pulled out the inventories to work on Bo's Monday morning grocery list.

But she couldn't concentrate. The Saguaro had never seemed so empty. She wished she'd been able to go with Bobby, with Frank. The Saturday night rides every other week were part of the fabric of her life, part of the routine that held things together. And Frank had become part of that fabric, without her even realizing it.

She stood up, paced the length of the café, then back again. She paused at the old jukebox, fumbled for a quarter and punched C7 without thinking. Hank Williams.

As soon as the music started, Kate knew she'd made a mistake. The melancholy tones turned the atmosphere downright desolate. She leaned her head against the glass case and closed her eyes. Frank hadn't said he'd come to Sunday dinner. The list of jobs was complete. He could be gone by tomorrow.

The song was ending when Bobby burst into the café. "Mom! You won't believe what me and Frank found. Coyote pups! Frank says to hurry before the mother gets back."

The two horses stood quietly beneath the Saguaro's sign. Frank stood between them.

Bobby ran to mount the smaller horse. At the boy's sudden motion, Blaze snorted, shook out his black mane and pulled hard against the reins. Frank held them fast and spoke softly. The big horse stilled and nuzzled his shoulder.

Kate moved as though in a dream. The Saguaro's sign flickered, throwing long emerald shadows.

Frank steadied the stirrup and gave Kate a hand up. His grip was firm. It grew even firmer as he swung himself up behind her and reached around her for the reins.

Bobby's horse's hoofbeats signaled the way. Frank followed with Kate, nudging Blaze into an easy gait.

She should have known what the feel of his body so close to hers would do, his touch, his smell. All of it brought back the hunger she'd felt since that night on the porch with a sudden, crushing immediacy.

"It's not far," he said, his voice smooth in her ear. She thought of the way his voice had set her heart pounding when he'd bent at the jukebox that first day.

The horse lurched and Frank's hand tightened on her stomach. One thumb brushed her breast. Kate sucked in her breath and leaned forward, burying her hands in the thick, coarse mane.

But her hips sensed every muscle that moved in his thighs, and her calves felt the pressure of his knees. When she finally straightened, the beat of his heart against her spine set up a rhythm in her body that seemed to control even the number of breaths she drew. His hand shifted again. Fire bloomed in Kate's belly.

She tried to focus on the moon and time its emergence from the clouds. She tried to fill her lungs with the fragrance of the flowers and the cooling sand. She tried to hear only the sturdy *clop, clop* of the horses' hooves on the sand-packed trail.

But the hard muscles moved in his arms as Frank tightened the reins, and that drew all her attention. Kate smelled his rich scent, heard him breathe in deeply each time she shifted her weight.

When they finally reached the mouth of the cave, the cavorting coyote pups were tumbling over one another, their short high barks signaling a would-be warning. She laughed, sharing Bobby's joy, but it was like watching a homemade video—watching herself with Bobby, watching Frank with Bobby, watching the pups, the moon, the deepening night. She was there, but something else was really happening, something over which she had no control, *wanted* no control.

On the return trip they played their usual game of guessing the shadowy-shaped cactus—ocotillo with its long slender arms, short fat barrel, crazy, fuzzy-armed cholla. Kate was surprised that her voice was steady, that her guesses were accurate.

She'd given up avoiding leaning back into Frank's chest. Now her shoulders matched the sway of his shoulders, her hips the rocking of his in the saddle as Blaze moved forward. And all the while her blood ran so hot in her veins she hardly felt the chill of the cooling desert air.

Mattie was waiting underneath the cactus sign when they returned. It seemed to Kate just a moment later that Mattie and Bobby were racing up the path to the house, that she was sliding out of the saddle and climbing onto Bobby's horse, that they'd covered the short mile trek back to the neighboring ranch.

She hadn't asked Frank to come along, help her rub down the horses, walk back with her in the moonlight. But as they waved a goodbye to the rancher and retraced the dusty road to the highway, it occurred to Kate that she hadn't asked because it hadn't been necessary. He knew she wanted him to come. And she knew that he would do it, knew he would ease his stride to match hers, knew that when they reached the gate over the cattle guard, he would stop, as he was stopping now, and draw her into his arms.

Then his lips met hers and the connection that had begun when she'd mounted the horse, perhaps even long before that, was finally complete...almost complete. Then knowing stopped and something else took over. Something wild and reckless.

They kissed for a lifetime it seemed, as though trying to touch something just out of reach. They kissed as eagerly as the wrens return to the prickly pear fruit in late summer and gorge on it, filling their bodies near to bursting with the sweet, rich fruit.

He moved his hands down her shoulders, down her spine where it had pressed against his chest as they'd ridden, down and over her hips that had rubbed against the inside of his thighs, driving him mad with wanting her.

And her hands answered, light at first, then firmer, then bolder than he'd dared imagine.

The moon disappeared and took time with it. The smell, the taste, the touch of her body filled all of Frank's senses, filled him completely, almost completely....

How long had they stood at the gate, his mouth exploring, hers yielding hungrily at each new onslaught?

When had they moved down the highway, stopping when they had to for another taste?

When had the rain begun? It had drenched them both, till their clothing seemed but a second skin.

Only when Frank took her hand and they raced across the swirling puddles in the café's parking lot did real time click back into focus for Kate. *Home.*

Then it seemed forever before he unlocked the door to his room and led her inside. Forever before they could peel off each other's wet, clinging shirts. Forever before her breasts swung free and his hands were on them, caressing, warming.

Then the bed was beneath her, the sheets smooth against her back, his hands moving down to stroke her jean-clad thighs. He kissed her belly and the hollows at her waist, following the trail of his fingers till she groaned and called out his name and pulled him back to her mouth.

She'd never get enough, Kate thought. Never taste enough, never touch enough to stop the trembling that had seized her. She arched her body.

It didn't matter that they still wore jeans. The brush of her hips against his was enough. A sound came out of him then. No words. Just a long, low rumble of pleasure. It tore down through his chest to tighten his gut then plunge to the aching pressure below it.

The feeling pitched Frank out of control, the same way wind used to tear around the racetrack, bringing a fine, blinding grit, rendering him helpless till he could tear at the layered breakaway face mask to clear his vision. He saw sharply then. If he could get back in control, he'd see sharply now. Frank opened his eyes. Kate filled his vision.

Kate. Not one of the superficial women who showed up at the track on race day, claiming to have saved themselves for the thrill of being bedded by a man who drove fast cars, or better yet, was rich enough to own them. This was Kate, who didn't even know who he was, who probably wouldn't care if she did know. *Kate.* Fair against the white sheet, his own darker body a shadow over hers, her light hair a tangle on the pillow.

Her body arched again toward his, as yielding as an opening flower, as full of softness and passion as the women he'd known had been hard and cold. It had been easy to maintain his control with them. A meeting of bodies, but never of hearts.

But this woman...*this* woman...he stroked Kate's hips, moving her lower till she was beneath him.

She reached out and touched him then through the taut fabric of his jeans. And Frank imagined the terrible force of his own unrestrained passion. So easy to love her. *Too easy to hurt her.*

The rain had stopped. The only sound was the slow drip of water down the gutter, the soft keening of the woman beneath him, the rasp of his breath and the thunder of his heart.

He had no choice. He would risk it and hope that he really had changed.

Frank reached for the half-undone zipper of his jeans. As he did it, the thunder of his heart became a distant rumble.

It turned into a metallic roar.

The sound grew deafening, then exploded into fragments, each heavy engine shredding the stillness, till the small room shook with a bursting vibration of noise.

Frank swung off the bed. A crazy-quilt pattern of flashing lights swept through the curtained window, crossed his bare chest and spun off the walls. The lights disappeared. The sound faded. Then it all began again.

In the strobe-lit semidarkness he saw Kate fumble for her shirt, find his, pull it on. He moved toward the window. "They're circling the café," he said over the din.

"It's Bo's rowdy motorcycle friends. He'll be mad as the dickens when they wake him up." Her voice shook, belying her offhand words.

When she joined him at the window, Frank drew her back. Her body was warm to his protective touch, and fragrant. Then the roar of the motorcycles rose again, and three headlamp beams spun crazily off the walls of the room.

When they'd passed he looked out the window again. "Whoever they are, they're worse than rowdy," he said. "The tall one's dead drunk. It's a wonder he's still on the bike. The other two aren't much better. Stay here. Keep the door locked."

Kate shivered in the darkness. The damp chambray shirt clung to her breasts with a clammy, cold tenacity. Her fingers moved clumsily over the buttons.

Then she heard the cycles spin in the gravel in the front parking lot. Around and around they went, their drivers issuing war whoops and rebel yells. A scatter of stones hit the Saguaro's front window. The yelling grew louder. Then more spinning, more stones.

Damn it, she would *not* replace another piece of cracked plate glass. She'd go out there and stop this here and now. She'd faced a lot worse in the past ten years without being beaten. Kate jerked open the door.

An iron hand closed around her arm and pulled her toward the shadow at the corner of the building. "I *told* you to stay in the room!" Frank's voice was harsh above the roar of the motorcycle engines.

"They're Bo's old friends. I've dealt with them before."

Another round of gravel pelted the glass. Kate pulled free. "The café is all I've got and I *won't* have it vandalized. I'll cross the lot, go in the back door and call the state police."

She'd taken half a dozen steps, Frank close on her heels, when the cycles rounded the café again.

Something about the shortest man was familiar, Kate thought. Then the headlamps blinded her.

A string of obscenities split the exhaust-laden air. Kate stiffened. These weren't Bo's friends, but she knew one voice. The short man was the young would-be highway worker that Bo had thrown out of the café last week.

Frank's voice was low in her ear. "I'm going to head toward the garage. Just stay where you are. They'll follow me."

"But I don't think—"

"*Just do as I say.*"

He moved her aside and strode across the parking lot toward the bikers, his hands at his sides, fingers splayed. The muscles in his back shone tense and gleaming in the cactus sign's glow.

The bikers waited, engines revving, watching till he'd drawn even with the café. Then two of them moved steadily toward him. Their bikes pinned Frank against the small side window.

Kate sprinted forward, heading for the Saguaro's back door, but the short man throttled down his engine, spun out and slid between her and the building.

Kate froze, the young man's eyes inches away. They darted over her body like small black bugs looking for a place to land. She could smell stale sweat and the antiseptic odor of gin.

"Wanna go for a ride, babe? Bet I could take you places you ain't never been before."

Frank lurched forward and snarled out something she couldn't hear. The two bikers cut their engines, turned and stared over their shoulders.

Nausea rose in Kate's throat. She forced it down with rage. "Get off my property, mister, or all you'll see is the the inside of the Summit City jail."

They were bullies. She'd seen worse. But her legs felt like jelly as she forced them forward, toward Frank.

The short man dismounted. He grabbed her arm as she passed him. She tried to wrench free but the man held her fast.

"Lay off the woman," the big, burly biker said. Then the tall, thin man half slid, half dismounted and kicked the bike stand three times before it came down. He took a lurching step forward. The short man let go of Kate's arm.

The thin biker stood almost as tall as Frank. "We hear you do good work, mister. Hear you know somethin' 'bout bikes."

Frank hooked his thumbs in his pockets. "You've got the wrong man, buddy. Try further down the road."

The burly biker pulled nicotine-stained fingers through a scraggly beard. "Ain't no sense in that. You got a garage. You got tools. Don't matter if you ain't the guy we heard about."

"We're closed," Frank said.

"Now that's mighty strange. The light's still burning. Y'all sure are trusting, leavin' things so inviting at night."

The short biker's eyes jumped back to Kate. Frank stiffened.

The tall biker had moved off and over toward the cactus sign. He was staring up at the pulsing neon and weaving, transfixed. The short man turned away to start his bike. That left only the big, burly biker. With just a little luck... Frank sidestepped the man and pivoted toward the Saguaro's front door, pulling Kate with him.

"I heard you pull up," he said over his shoulder. "I didn't hear signs of engine trouble."

"Ain't nothin' wrong with our machines," the biker said. "We ain't here for no spring tune-up. We want to go *fast*. We hear you're the man for the job."

"Yeah, we want to go fast. *Real* fast." The short kid had given up fooling with his bike and was cleaning his fingernails with a knife that looked long enough to skin a deer. "We want to *fly,* " he said. He waved the knife through the air for emphasis.

Beneath his grip on her shoulder, Frank felt Kate tremble.

The burly biker followed Kate's terrified gaze and shouted a curse word at his friend. "Put yer toy away, kid. We don't want to scare the little lady."

"Come back tomorrow," Frank said coolly. He opened the screen and nudged Kate toward it. She fumbled in her pocket for her keys.

"Nice tattoo on your shoulder, there." The tall biker had returned. Now he lurched forward for a closer look. "Ain't never seen no tattoo like that."

The short man moved forward, balancing the knife on his palm. "Looks like a chicken to me. Wonder what kinda guy'd get a chicken put on his shoulder, huh? You *chicken*, mister?"

Kate had the key and was working it into the lock.

''Rooster's got a mighty pretty little hen. Too bad he hasn't got the guts to keep 'er.''

Kate stumbled into the café. Frank pulled the door closed after her, then stepped out, forcing the bikers forward. He crouched low, his arms curved at his sides, the blood already pounding hard in his fists, throbbing in his neck, ringing in his ears.

They were on him in a minute.

Chapter Six

"Just *hurry*," Kate screamed into the receiver. Mac kept asking for details, all the while assuring her that the cruiser was less than ten miles away.

"Ten miles means ten minutes. Frank could be *dead* in that length of time. I saw the blade on that biker's knife."

Kate slammed down the receiver just as something hard hit the front plate glass window. A long, jagged crack shot diagonally from corner to corner. The man in the black leather vest slid down the glass, groaning.

Kate ran to the window just as Bo lumbered across the street. Moments later the shiny length of steel jumped out of the short biker's fist, went up in the air and came down on the cement porch. Bo kicked the knife closer to the door.

Kate pushed the screen open and grabbed for the weapon, her knuckles skinning on the cement. She backed into the darkened café, clutching the knife to her chest. At a touch on her shoulder she spun around.

Mattie was too terrified to speak.

"Mom, what's going on?" Bobby said, moving toward the front window.

Kate jerked him back. "Take Mattie to the dish room and lock the door. Don't come out till I tell you."

Bobby's eyes widened as he looked from the knife to his mother's face, then out at the struggling men. "But, Mom—"

"*Go*, Bobby! *Now*."

Mattie grabbed the boy's hand and hurried him off. In the distance a siren screamed.

Kate turned back. It was two against two now, Frank and the tall biker, Bo and the heavier man. The shorter man who'd dropped the knife was stumbling toward his bike.

The burly biker put up a strong fight, but his reach was short. Bo managed to dance out of the way, avoiding at least every third punch. He got in a few licks of his own, though his drunk opponent seemed not to feel a thing.

Finally Bo lowered his head, gave out a great roar and butted the biker in the stomach. The bandy legs buckled and the man went down. Bo sat down on him, hard.

"You're squashing me, man. Get the hell off," the biker whined.

"That's what we do with bugs around here. Ain't you learned that yet?"

With Frank it was an entirely different matter. The tall biker kept coming at him, fists bared, and Frank kept knocking him down. He swung with his left fist, his right arm hanging limp at his side.

Then suddenly the biker seemed to make a mental connection. He came at Frank hard from the right. Frank staggered, then went to his knees. Kate's stomach rolled over.

The noise of the siren grew deafening. Then a circle of blinding white light held them all. The biker swayed and shielded his eyes. Frank struggled to get back on his feet.

No, Kate thought, *don't get up.* She clutched the knife in her hand more tightly, aware for the first time of the sticky ooze and the sharp scent of blood. With a start she realized the meaning of Frank's left-handed jabs and useless right arm.

He tried to get up again. Kate screamed and crashed out through the door.

Frank heard the terror in Kate's voice through the pounding blood in his ears. *If one of these animals has gotten his hands on her. . .* He struck out, hard.

Punch followed punch with uncontrolled rage. The biker fell heavily to his knees. Frank reached for his collar to pull him up. A viselike grip closed over his wrist. The hard barrel of a shotgun jabbed into his gut.

"It's over," Mac said.

Frank stared at the trooper, then down at the biker. The man was crying like a baby. On the fringe of his consciousness, he heard the roar of a departing motorcycle.

Kate shoved the gun away. "What are you *doing,* Mac? These men tried to kill Frank. One of them is getting away. And this . . . this *lowlife—*"

"Let's all just calm down, now, shall we?"

Calm down. Frank had heard that often enough. Usually in the aftermath of a Vincenti free-for-all. His gaze swung from the trooper's tense face to Kate's distraught one, over to Bo, Mattie clinging to him and crying, then down into the blood-smeared face of his opponent. He'd wanted to kill the man. He might have done it. He couldn't even remember why.

Frank pulled free and headed for the cruiser.

"Don't anybody else go anywhere," Mac said. He hitched up his pants and followed after Frank.

"You'll have to come into the city to swear out a warrant," Mac said. "I'll get some backup to go after the one who got away." He switched off the revolving strobe light and reached for the mike. "Let's hear what happened."

Frank was silent.

Mac drew his face close to Frank's. "Look, buddy, don't get smart with me. I know my business. There's always more than meets the eye, even a trained one like my own."

"I don't want to press charges. Check with Kate."

"You *what?*"

"These morons rode in here looking for a fight. They got one. They won't be back."

"Nice gash you got on your arm."

"I've had worse."

"What the hell are you hiding, Vincenti?"

"Nothing that would interest you."

"Try me."

Again Frank was silent.

The trooper hung the mike back in its cradle, and Frank turned away, toward the garage.

"I'll find out sooner or later," the trooper called after him.

By the time you do, I'll be long gone. Frank pushed open the office door and slammed it behind him.

Bobby was wide-awake, insisting on details. "What kind of knife was it, Mom? How come you had to give it back to MacMillan? What'll he do with it?"

"Bobby Prescott, if you don't lie down this minute, I'm going to ground you for a week. And don't you ever leave the house again when there's trouble at the café. You scared Mattie half to death tearing off like that."

"Aw, Mom." Bobby sank back against the pillows and yawned, then started up again. "Frank did really good, didn't he, Mom? Bo says he held off all three of them."

"No more, Bobby, please. We'll talk about it tomorrow."

She crossed the room and leaned against the door till Bobby's even breathing told her he was sleeping.

Mattie was curled up on the couch. She'd seen to Bo's blackening eyes, then begged to stay up at the house with Kate. "It drives him nuts to see me like this," she had said. "I go all jelly-kneed when that man gets hurt."

She'd done the same, Kate thought moments later, as she pulled a blanket over Mattie's sleeping form, then stepped out onto the porch. But she'd have jumped on that biker herself if he'd hit Frank one more time.

Still, it was the biker's tearstained, bloodied face upturned to Frank's raging one that kept appearing before her. She shook her head to clear the vision and headed down the path, the first-aid kit swinging from its strap on her shoulder.

The light was out in his room and the curtains were drawn. Kate knocked softly on the door.

No answer.

She knocked again. "Frank, it's me. Are you all right?"

There was a stirring and the creak of bedsprings as he got up off the mattress. A moment later he pulled open the door.

"Your arm—"

"I found gauze and iodine in the garage."

"Mac says you should get a tetanus shot."

"I'll take care of it in the morning. On my way out. I'm leaving, Kate."

His eyes were as hard as his words, his tone as determined as it had been that first evening he'd come to the café. Nothing that had happened between them, nothing she'd said or done had made any difference. And if there was one thing Kate had learned well, it was that a man could not be held by a woman's need.

"Good night, Frank," she said quietly. "I'll have your wages ready in the morning."

She turned away but he caught her arm. "It's all the same, Kate. Rage. Passion for anything. My father's blood runs as hot and as thick in my veins as it ever ran in my brother's. Jesse's dead. But there will be no more casualties, by God."

He let her go and stepped back into the darkened room.

Frank stood at the closed door long after Kate's footsteps had faded. The silence that remained seemed bottomless. Then the throbbing in his arm grew intolerable. He stretched out on the bed facedown, his arm in the trough of ice he'd fashioned with bath towels.

The bleeding had stopped quickly enough after he'd taped the gash closed. Now there was only the pain. He was grateful for it. If he thought about his arm, he wouldn't think of Kate.

It was good that he was going. What would she have said if she'd known that he didn't need her money or her job? That he'd always been guarded with women but never dishonest. That he'd never misled anyone in his life . . . till now.

She'd followed him out of the room when he'd told her to stay behind. He remembered his sudden flash of anger. What if he ever got angry at her the way he had at the biker? She had the power, the fire, the passion to provoke him, he knew.

A sharp, hot pain shot up his arm, leaving him dizzy. Frank clinched ice cubes in his fist till they splintered.

He had never laid a hand on a woman. But there were other ways to hurt. Angry words, stubborn acts, betrayal, abandonment. Even sex. A man could get carried away. Things could get out of hand. He'd always been careful to hold himself back. But what he'd felt for Kate tonight—this mixture of heat and desire and something far deeper—this was different. If ever he lay with her again . . .

Frank rolled to his back as his roused desire battled with the pain in his arm and the spinning in his head.

To take her like that, no holds barred, to press his body and hers to the limit, to lose himself totally... he knew he'd never be able to stop it once it began, no more than he'd been able to control his rage at the biker.

There'd be no more casualties, he'd promised. Not if he had to run forever. He'd go to his grave unchanged.

The morning sun slanted in at a crazy angle through the cracked front window of the Saguaro Café.

"It wasn't like that at all," Bobby tried to tell his teacher. "It was a *real* fight, not like in the movies. One guy had a knife and Frank got cut bad, but he just kept on till MacMillan came. He had to spend all day yesterday resting up. Lucky for him it was Sunday. Ain't that right, Bo?"

The big cook shrugged and went on turning pancakes.

"The proper word is *isn't,* Bobby," Ev White said. "There's no such word as *ain't.* "

The café was silent except for the sound of sizzling bacon on the griddle and the drip of the coffeepot.

"Nobody wants to talk about the fight," Bobby muttered. "It's the biggest thing that's happened at the crossing in ages. Bo ought to be proud of his shiner, and Mom's all embarrassed, like the fight was her fault. Everybody at school's going to think I made the whole thing up."

The café door swung open. Bobby grinned at the rancher who came through it. "See that crack in the window? Bet you can't guess how *that* happened."

"Bobby—"

"When Frank gets here I'm going to get him to show me that left hook he used. Boy, if I ever get into a fight—"

"*Bobby!* A fistfight is nothing to be proud of, young man. It's senseless and dangerous."

"And downright *common*," Ev added.

Bobby made a face at his teacher. "You're all against Frank. Just 'cause he's not a sissy."

Kate picked up Bobby's empty plate and put it on the tray, then gave him another glass of ice water as if he'd just sat down instead of already finished eating. She'd been doing things like that all morning, she realized.

"Nobody's against Frank, Bobby. But what you saw Saturday night was not a good example of how to settle arguments."

"And certainly not something for an impressionable young boy to witness," Ev added.

Bobby pushed away from the table. "I'm *not* a little kid. I'm almost ten. I saw what I saw, and I think Frank was right. And when I grow up..." Kate glared at her son. "When I grow up I'm going to fight when I have to, and be good at fixing things, and stretch every morning so I'll be tall, and—"

"Bobby, *please*. I don't want to hear another word about what happened. And you'd better start doing your homework right after school from now on. You've been spending entirely too much time in that garage."

"I aced the test, just like I promised Frank."

"And you'll have to learn to work by yourself. Frank's leaving this morning."

"You *fired* him?"

"No. He told me after the . . . disturbance that he intends to go."

Bobby stared at his mother. Mattie looked up from the counter. Bo had turned, his shiner as dark as the short stack of pancakes burning on the griddle.

Bobby kicked the leg of the table so hard Ev White's coffee sloshed into her saucer. "It isn't *fair*. He wouldn't go if you said not to, Mom. I know he wouldn't."

The school bus rolled into the parking lot, and Bobby grabbed his book bag. He hit the door just as Frank came through it, dressed in his suit, his backpack over his shoulder. Bobby took one look and ran for the bus.

"Need a lift into town?" Bo mumbled. "I'll be goin' in later for groceries."

"No, thanks," Frank said. "I've got a ride." He nodded toward a trucker who was just getting up to pay his bill.

Mattie pushed a cup of coffee across the counter. "Don't you want breakfast? Won't take but a minute to fry up some—"

"No."

At the single stern word, all eyes turned his direction. Everyone waited.

Kate took an envelope from her apron pocket and held it out.

He shook his head.

"Please. Take it."

"You don't owe me anything. I told you before."

"You've brought the café and the rooms up to par."

"I've brought you nothing but trouble." He turned toward the door.

"Those biker bullies aren't the worst thing I've seen in the middle of this godforsaken place, Frank Vincenti."

He turned around. "If Newton's Crossing is so godforsaken, why the hell do you stay?"

Kate set the tray down on the counter. "I happen to think that a person can't run away from herself, or *himself,* that's why."

He adjusted his dark glasses, worked his jaw and shifted the backpack up on his shoulder. The screen door swung closed behind him without a sound.

Good riddance. Kate tried to say the words, but she knew if she did, she'd cry instead.

All at once everybody got up to pay. She checked out the trucker, the rancher, a scattering of customers. It was like being in the condolence line at Pop's funeral. Their faces held sympathy though no one said a word.

Except Ev White, who leaned over the register and whispered, "Now you know what it feels like to be left behind in the dust." Ev spun around, her low heels tapping on the hard linoleum as she headed for the door.

Bo was scraping burned pancake off the griddle. Mattie was heading down the counter to avoid him.

Kate took off her apron and tossed it onto the counter. "I have to go up to the house. I'll be back in an hour."

"Take your time. *We* ain't goin' nowhere," Bo said. He touched her arm as she passed him. Kate felt the tears rise. She had to get out before they fell.

Frank leaned against the side of the truck, waiting for the driver. The faded cardboard Help Wanted sign still sat in the garage window, but at least, thanks to Bobby, the glass was clean now. So were the bays. He and Bo had worked at them off and on all week.

Across the street the Saguaro's parking lot was emptying. Kate had forgotten to turn off the cactus sign. Where would he be when she remembered? Las Vegas? Barstow? Someplace farther west? He could see her slender fingers reaching for the switch.

Beyond, Rock Top Mountain cast a long shadow on the empty highway. At its dark edge a lone bird circled then dropped to examine the leavings of the dawn. Not a soaring falcon, he knew. Most likely, a vulture. He looked back toward the café.

Funny how a whole world, a whole lifetime could exist in a few scattered buildings in the middle of nowhere. In a week he'd been no farther from the crossing than the one-mile walk to the ranch the night they'd taken the horses back.

The memory grabbed him in his gut and twisted . . . the feel of her body, the smell of her. Now he was going to pay. Pay with intolerable memories and the knowledge that there'd never be another night in his life like that one, no chance to finish what he had started, never another woman like Kate.

The trucker climbed into the cab and he followed. At the sound of the mighty engine rolling over, a restless urge swept through Frank's body. It shot down his arms and into his hands.

He wanted to drive. For the first time in years, he *wanted* to put his hands to the wheel of something small and powerful and dangerous and go very, very fast. So fast he'd forget her face forever. Forget he'd ever tasted her lips, forget he'd ever set foot in Newton's Crossing, Nevada. Population five. Kate, Mattie, Bo and—

"Bobby!"

The semi's brakes screamed as the small boy darted across the road. The trucker swore and turned white.

Frank leaned out the window. "Bobby, what the hell—"

"If you stay, I promise not to bug you anymore about the derby car."

Bobby's tears had made dusty tracks down his flushed cheeks. He hung on to the mirror and the door as though the weight of his body could keep the big truck from moving.

"There's nothing in California, Frank. I been there once."

"Bobby, you're not the reason I'm going. What happened Saturday night—"

"That wasn't your fault. I tried to tell them. I tried to tell Mom, but she wouldn't listen."

"It's not her fault, either, kid."

"It *is*. I know it is. Frank, take me with you. I take back what I said about California."

"Your mother needs you, kid. You get in there and tell her how much *you* need *her*."

At Frank's sudden sharp tone, Bobby dropped to the running board and then to the ground. He stepped backward, his small fists clinched at his sides.

"Go on then. I don't care. I don't care if you *never* come back."

The trucker threw the shift in gear. "Got to get this rig on the road."

Frank nodded and the trucker revved the engine. The semi lurched forward, paused at the light and then turned.

Frank stared out the dusty front window, his shoulders rigid. Ahead was the long, winding ribbon of highway, the mountain in the distance, the coast beyond that.

Pacific means peaceful.

Everything in him wrenched at the memory of Kate's words, and Bobby's. His eyes moved to the side view mirror. Behind was a house on a hill, a scattering of stucco buildings, a woman he could not see, would never see again. And a small defiant boy, standing in the dust at the side of the road.

Frank closed his eyes, but he could not erase the images. "I've got to go back," he said to the trucker.

"You forget something, mister?"

"Yeah," Frank said. "I don't know what the hell it is, but I damn well better go back and find out."

Even before he'd swung himself out of the truck, Bobby was cutting through the desert, running full speed to meet him. On the edge of the highway the boy stumbled forward. "I knew you wouldn't leave."

The tall man bent down. "You knew a heck of a lot more than I did, kid."

"I guess we're even. You helped me with math. I helped you decide."

Frank took hold of Bobby's shoulders. "There's something you have to try to understand. I'm here. That's it. No promises, no guarantees. I don't know what the outcome of all this will be."

"Like a race? Like when you start out. You don't know how it's going to end. You build the car and try to make it fast, but you don't know if you've got a chance to win."

Bobby was talking about his derby car, but he'd drawn a blueprint of Frank's entire life. You built the car. You trusted that it would all come out right in the end. You kept the faith. He'd done it with machines. Why the hell couldn't he do it with himself?

Bobby kicked at the dust. "I promised not to mention the derby car."

Frank tipped the boy's chin. "You've missed the school bus, kid."

"Yeah, I told 'em a fib. Said I was going in with Miss White."

Frank stood up and looked down the road. "The lady's car is still in the parking lot."

"I guess I'd better get going."

Frank shifted his bag to his shoulder. Then Bobby reached up and took his hand.

The telephone rang, shattering the silence in the house on the hill. Kate blew her nose and waited eight rings while she screwed up the courage to go into the kitchen and pick up the receiver.

"He's back. He wants to see you," Mattie said.

It would only mean another goodbye, possibly a more painful one. So why did she want to rush down the hill and say she didn't care, say she wouldn't think about tomorrow and that neither should he?

"Kate?"

"I'll be right down, Mattie."

She splashed water on her face and dried it, hard. He was back and she didn't know why. It didn't matter. He was back.

Moments later, metal banging against metal rang out as Kate stepped into the garage. The air seemed to vibrate and seep into her body. A canary yellow hot rod was up on the lifts. Frank, his back to her, was working under it.

When had the lifts been repaired? And when had he found time to paint the cinder block walls, replace the overhead lights, sweep and wash the cement floor? It wasn't the same garage.

Frank's eyes lit with a momentary flash of hot bright blue when he saw her. Then they grew distant. Not trusting her voice, Kate glanced up toward the row of high, clean windows.

"I thought you'd have better luck hiring a mechanic if things were in shape," he said carefully. "Now...maybe there's no need."

Grease from his hands left dark smudges on the Help Wanted sign he passed her. "I'm applying for the job. If you'll have me."

"You...do you have any references?"

"Some guys in Indiana, Bo. After Saturday night I'm not sure about Mattie."

"What I said about running...I had no right."

"You had every right. I've been running all my life."

From what? she knew she should ask him. "There are things we should settle," she said instead.

"I'll lease the garage for six months, replenish the stock, do some advertising with what I make on the hot rod. We'll split any future profits fifty-fifty."

Six months, she thought. *Almost forever.*

"I'll need a telephone," he said.

"I'll get it hooked up right away."

"It's a deal, then?" He stretched out a hand. Kate met it immediately.

The grease slid from his palm to hers. They laughed, then, lingered in it, dispelling the last of the tension. Finally Frank reached for a towel hanging from a peg and passed it to her.

"I'll send Bo over with the key to your room," she said. "And you're welcome in the Saguaro for meals, as always."

She stood still, waiting, letting him study her face. "I'd like to pay from now on," he said. "For the room, for meals, for whatever else comes along. We'll ... do it differently." He nodded, all business, and moved back to the car.

"See you at lunch, then," Kate said. Already at work beneath the car's hood, he didn't answer.

The sun was bright and she had to squint as she crossed the street. He was telling her that the wall he'd brought to the crossing was up again. It didn't matter. She'd torn it down once, she'd do it again. In six months she could do *anything*.

* * *

The morning moved swiftly. Before Frank knew it Bo had appeared at the garage and was shoving a sandwich and a handful of orders his way.

"Word got out quick that you was staying, Frank. Seems like folks been saving up their problems, waitin' till this particular garage reopened. Even Mac's bragging about the cruiser. And me and Mattie went into Summit City one night . . . course we didn't promote the garage to exactly the right people."

"Don't worry about it, those bikers won't be back." Frank shuffled through the orders. "Can we get credit at the parts store in Summit City?"

"The Newton name still carries its weight in auto stores clear to the border. Even though your name don't match, you won't get any static."

At the door Bo paused and tugged at his ponytail. "Uh, Frank, when you get back to your room, don't blame me. There's a floor lamp with a fussy-lookin' shade, a big easy chair, even one of them little refrigerators and a hot plate. Kate had me movin' stuff all morning."

"She didn't have to do that."

"You shoulda seen what she done for Mattie and me when we first settled into the trailer." Bo rubbed a big hand slowly down the wooden frame of the door. "She makes you feel like family. She don't ask nothin' in return." He slapped the frame and went outside. "It's gonna be hot," he said. "You better start up the garage swamp cooler."

Bo was right, Frank thought as the afternoon wore on. Giving was a part of Kate's nature. Another part emerged when it came to passion. Some fortunate man, someday in the future, would find out all about that.

But not him. He flexed his arm under the bandage and let the dull ache of the healing wound shoot all the way down to his fingers. He knew what he was now, knew he hadn't changed. The only thing he wasn't sure of was why he had stayed. Bobby. Kate. Himself?

Chapter Seven

Mornings had been nothing less than chaotic. Today seemed worse. In the dish room Kate crowded
glasses of orange juice onto a tray for the breakfast
crowd waiting out front.

If business would only slow, she could check with
Frank about fixing the front window, about . . . other
things. She thought of the day they'd washed that
window, a transparent wall between them. They'd
been so close, yet so far apart. Like now.

He'd been up to his neck in work for a week.

"That's no excuse for not eating," she'd told him
Monday night.

He'd seemed distracted, though his eyes had flashed
with those penetrating silver sparks. For a moment
she'd felt a direct connection between his heart and

NO COST! NO OBLIGATION TO BUY!
NO PURCHASE NECESSARY!

PLAY "LUCKY 7"
AND GET FIVE FREE GIFTS!

HOW TO PLAY:

1. With a coin, carefully scratch off the silver box at the right. Then check the claim chart to see what we have for you—FREE BOOKS and a gift—ALL YOURS! ALL FREE!

2. Send back this card and you'll receive brand-new Silhouette Special Edition® novels. These books have a cover price of $3.99 each, but they are yours to keep absolutely free.

3. There's no catch. You're under no obligation to buy anything. We charge nothing—ZERO—for your first shipment. And you don't have to make any minimum number of purchases—not even one!

4. The fact is thousands of readers enjoy receiving books by mail from the Silhouette Reader Service™ months before they're available in stores. They like the convenience of home delivery and they love our discount prices!

5. We hope that after receiving your free books you'll want to remain a subscriber. But the choice is yours—to continue or cancel, anytime at all! So why not take us up on our invitation, with no risk of any kind. You'll be glad you did!

This beautiful porcelain box is topped with a lovely bouquet of porcelain flowers, perfect for holding rings, pins or other precious trinkets — and is yours absolutely free when you accept our no risk offer!

PLAY "LUCKY 7"

**Just scratch off the silver box with a coin.
Then check below to see the gifts you get.**

YES! I have scratched off the silver box. Please send me all the gifts for which I qualify. I understand I am under no obligation to purchase any books, as explained on the back and on the opposite page.

235 CIS A3JC
(U-SIL-SE-08/96)

NAME

ADDRESS   APT.

CITY   STATE   ZIP

 WORTH FOUR FREE BOOKS PLUS A FREE PORCELAIN TRINKET BOX

 WORTH THREE FREE BOOKS

 WORTH TWO FREE BOOKS

WORTH ONE FREE BOOK

Offer limited to one per household and not valid to current Silhouette Special Edition® subscribers. All orders subject to approval.

© 1990 HARLEQUIN ENTERPRISES LIMITED   **PRINTED IN U.S.A.**

THE SILHOUETTE READER SERVICE™: HERE'S HOW IT WORKS

Accepting free books places you under no obligation to buy anything. You may keep the books and gift and return the shipping statement marked "cancel". If you do not cancel, about a month later we'll send you 6 additional novels, and bill you just $3.34 each plus 25¢ delivery and applicable sales tax, if any.* That's the complete price–and compared to cover prices of $3.99 each–quite a bargain! You may cancel at any time, but if you choose to continue, every month we'll send you 6 more books, which you may either purchase at the discount price…or return to us and cancel your subscription.

*Terms and prices subject to change without notice. Sales tax applicable in N.Y.

If offer card is missing, write to: Silhouette Reader Service, 3010 Walden Ave, PO Box 1867, Buffalo, NY 14240-1867

BUSINESS REPLY MAIL

FIRST-CLASS MAIL   PERMIT NO. 717   BUFFALO, NY

POSTAGE WILL BE PAID BY ADDRESSEE

SILHOUETTE READER SERVICE
3010 WALDEN AVE
PO BOX 1867
BUFFALO NY 14240-9952

NO POSTAGE
NECESSARY
IF MAILED
IN THE
UNITED STATES

hers. Then he said something banal and reached for another wrench. She'd silently slipped away.

On Tuesday she'd barely caught sight of him all day. Late that night they stood and talked in the moonlight, Bobby between them. They chose their words with the same care they had taken all week not to move close enough to touch. Frank mentioned his problems with the inventory and the delay on parts for the hot rod. She spoke of her plans for adding a part-time cook now that Bo was helping out more at the garage. Bobby asked some vague question about the center of gravity in a car. Then they'd said good-night.

Wednesday she'd worked on the books till midnight, and Frank did the same in the garage.

The days were passing, Kate thought, and the distance between them was as wide as ever.

She shifted the tray and headed out to the café, moving down the counter to distribute the glasses of juice, knowing that when she reached the far end where Frank sat, the few words they'd share would most likely have to last all day.

But she ran out of orange juice halfway down, just before Ev. The teacher, surprisingly, didn't complain. In fact, Kate realized, Ev hadn't said a word all morning.

She was about to ask what was wrong when the squeal of brakes and a telltale *thump* sent heads craning toward the big front window.

"It's Officer MacMillan," Bobby said. "He sure looks mad."

A wide band of duct tape covered the window's crack, bisecting the scene outside. On one side sat

Mac's patrol car and a slack tow chain, on the other an ancient black sedan.

Car doors flew open and slammed, and a gray-haired woman almost as tall and thin as her husband marched into the café behind Mac.

"He didn't signal, Albert. He was supposed to signal when he was ready to stop. Up for right, out for a left and down—"

"Cars have automatic lights now, Lilly. The chain was so short we just couldn't see them. But I take complete responsibility, Officer. I insist—"

Mac raised a weary hand and pulled out a chair for the woman, then slapped two fives on the table. "Breakfast's on me, folks. Lunch, too, if it comes to that. Y'all order up whatever you like."

"Oh, but we couldn't—"

"Oh, yes, you could, ma'am. Official orders."

Kate brought coffee as the trooper sank down onto the stool next to Ev, who set about ignoring him completely.

"I've been out all night, for God's sake, Evy," he mumbled to the teacher. Ev's face softened. Kate refilled her cup and poured one for MacMillan.

When Kate came back with a plate of sausage and eggs, the trooper glanced up gratefully. Then his gaze moved down the counter to where Frank sat with Bobby.

Mac jabbed the air with his fork. "What did you do to the cruiser last week? Tighten loose wires or something? Thing runs pretty good. You had it less than an hour."

Frank shrugged.

"Come on, you must have done something."

"I made a minor adjustment on the timing."

Mac snorted. "Never much good at that sort of thing myself. Headwork is more *my* style." He glanced at Kate and grinned.

Frank closed Bobby's math book and handed it back to him, then started to rise.

"Just a minute," Mac said. "Got a job for you." He lowered his voice. "Mr. and Mrs. Senior Citizen over there haven't got a buck between them. They were headed down to Vegas to see their son when the buggy broke down and the old man discovered he'd forgotten his wallet. No license, no cash, and they've never used credit cards in their lives. The son doesn't have a phone, and they can't remember where he works."

"You want me to work on their car."

"Something like that. First you'll have to talk them into letting you do it. It took me half the night to get them to let me tow them to the crossing, and *I* had the uniform, the badge, the speech about being a public servant. You got nothing...if it's true you aren't even a real mechanic."

Frank worked a muscle at the back of his jaw. "What's wrong with the car?"

"How should I know? The guy says it just stopped."

"Any noise? Leaks?"

"It was the middle of the night, for Pete's sake. How could I see if something was leaking?"

MacMillan forked up the last of his egg, crossed to the door and shoved on a pair of new mirrored sunglasses. He waited, drawing the attention of everyone in the café. He nodded at the couple and then toward Frank.

"That fella over there will see to your car, folks. Now don't forget, when you get to Vegas, you get that license replaced, you hear?" Mac shot Frank a self-satisfied grin and headed out.

The elderly woman dabbed at her mouth with a corner of her napkin. "Albert's terribly fussy with his car. I do hope you know what you're doing, young man."

"Now, Lilly, we're in no position to be critical." Albert leaned toward Frank. "We'd appreciate it if you could just tell us what the trouble is, perhaps patch things up enough to get us going."

"I'll do what I can to get you rolling."

Moments later out in the garage, Bo looked over Frank's shoulder and whistled. "Ain't no way I could work on that antique baby."

"Nice restoration job, huh?"

"You think you can fix it?"

"Oh, yes. But my work is going to be noticeable. I had hoped to avoid that."

"So word gets out that you're damn good with engines. What's wrong with that? First thing you know we'll have business comin' out our ears. You might even need a *full-time* assistant. Like me, for instance. What with MacMillan spreadin' the word and Mattie blabbin' to those bikers about what you did to the starting mechanism on my bike—"

The look Frank shot the big man stopped him cold. "Okay, okay, so we can do without biker business."

"It's not that, Bo. I had hoped . . . look, I stopped at the crossing to slow things down."

"And you thought maybe the world would do likewise and just leave you alone? Man, life don't stop for nobody. It might slow for a minute, but sooner or later...hell, Frank, you got to go somewhere from here. It ain't too soon to start thinkin' about that.''

Frank gestured impatiently toward the old sedan. "You don't understand. A job like this could drag me back, *right* back where I was. This is *not* just an ordinary back country car—''

An empty oil can rolled across the floor of the garage and Frank looked up to see Kate running back across the road.

He caught up with her on the Saguaro's front porch. Tears swam in her eyes, turning them a hard, brittle emerald.

"Kate, listen to me. You don't understand—''

"What is there to understand? You said you'd stay six months. You never said much else. Maybe that should have mattered to me, but it didn't. But get one thing straight, Frank Vincenti, I never intended to *drag* you anywhere.''

"I was talking about the job on that old car, not you, not the job in general.''

"Why would this particular repair make a difference? Aren't they all just the same? Beneath your dignity, your fancy MIT skills, your—''

"*Nothing* in Newton's Crossing is beneath me, Kate.''

He could feel the pounding of her pulse at her wrist as he took it. An answering thunder began in his head.

"Newton's Crossing is not just some *ordinary* wide spot in the middle of the road where you can stop in and wipe your boots. Agreement or no agreement, six months is too long if it's one day longer than you want to be here. Whatever you want—''

"I don't know what the hell I want. Do you?"

He kissed her, hard. Short and fast and deep enough to leave them both breathless. Then he broke away and headed for the garage.

It was two o'clock before the café had cleared and Kate had a chance to speak to Mattie. "Look, I'm sorry I ran out on you again this morning."

Mattie kept on beating the biscuit batter.

"I don't know what got into me."

"The whole thing's obvious," Mattie said. "Only thing is, both of you are too darn stubborn to admit it."

"He'll fix a few cars and be on his way. He's made that quite clear."

"Maybe you've got it wrong, Kate. You said yourself that you're good at imagining things. Look out the window. Frank finished with the old folks' car. Half a dozen people hung around to be next. The work alone could hold him—"

"And then?"

"I saw the way he kissed you."

"He was angry, nothing more."

"Funny way of showing it. I heard what he said, too. What *do* you want, Kate? If you'd take off that ring, and let your hair down now and then—"

"Oh, Mattie, it's no use. I've grown so *ordinary*, just like the crossing, maybe like you said, to keep men away." Kate tugged at the thin gold band till it came off, and shoved it down in the pocket of her jeans.

"If you'd wear a dress sometimes—"

"And lipstick, makeup? You know I'm not good at that." But she was good at something, Kate thought.

She was good at nurturing, at letting a man go his own way. She could still do that, at least that.

Mattie was silent, dropping lumps of biscuit dough onto the baking sheet, pushing them off the spoon with her finger.

"Remember that night Bo wanted me to go for a ride on his bike? I told him he was nuts, but he didn't get mad and ride off by himself like he used to, Kate. He kept on asking me to come, nice like. We had ice cream at the all-night diner in Summit City, hung out, talked with some bikers. But when the language got rough, Bo brought me home."

Mattie picked up the bowl, then set it down again. "Since Frank's been here, Bo's got more self-respect."

"Bo's had plenty to be proud of all along. He's a darn good cook."

"He'd be a better mechanic. He never believed that till Frank showed up."

They'd all begun to change, Kate thought. Everybody was thinking about cars—Bo, Bobby, half her customers. And she was thinking of wearing dresses to work. All because of Frank. If he was going to leave, he should do it now, before they all changed so much they couldn't snap back, before they all began to believe, like Mattie, that things at the crossing could be better just by being different.

What was the sense in having roots, she'd begun to wonder, if what grew above them was hardly recognizable?

Frank fumbled in the darkness for the chain to the overhead bulb. In the dim cast of light, he stripped off his grease-stained shirt and bent over the small shop basin.

He'd worked fast and hard, using the coping mechanism that had never failed him—work of any kind, as long as it had to do with cars. And the old car had turned out to be child's play. Tracing the intricate maze of wiring that sent the spark from the battery to the plugs and on to roll over the antique engine had been like a treasure hunt. He'd even found himself working up engine designs in his head again. He felt like a kid at camp after a long hard school year.

And the knowing had settled in then. Maybe cars *could* go on being a part of his life. Not racing, not the crazy life that had destroyed his family. Just cars that carried people to work and school. Just cars. And Kate.

Suddenly, out of nowhere, he felt again the yielding of her mouth under his. Everything stopped, as it had off and on all afternoon. His hands wouldn't move. That was another kind of knowing. One that he couldn't put into words because he didn't have them yet.

In the cracked mirror over the basin he imagined her face, imagined again the look she'd worn when she'd turned from him in anger.

If only he could explain to her as clearly as he'd explained to his lawyer when he'd phoned him in Indiana that morning. *I'm in Nevada. I'm working on cars. I'm planning on staying awhile.*

The race car was nearly ready for the Long Beach season opener. "A strong performance will push up the bidding," his lawyer had said, his tone jubilant.

"I'll get on the sale as soon as it's over. Come out to the coast. See the race, bring the lady."

He'd refused. Frank turned off the water and wiped his face with a towel. Taking Kate to an auto race made no more sense than kissing her had. No more sense than the aimless imagining he'd done all week about a future that might have been if he hadn't lost control with the bikers. But maybe...

Moments later, at the sound of the screen swinging open, she turned in his direction. Frank reached for words, but she turned her back and kept on stacking the dishes.

"The café's closed," Kate said. "I should have turned the sign around."

"I'm not hungry."

She reached for the last cup and stretched toward the shelf. Her hand was trembling.

His hand closed over hers. The ring was gone. He felt its absence. A hot, rough brush of heat shot down his body. "That shelf needs lowering," he said, his voice husky. "I'll take care of it as soon as I can."

She held the cup. He did not let go.

Time moved backward, then, to the moment he'd first seen her face when she'd poured his coffee. He took the cup from her and placed it on the shelf, then turned her to face him.

"I've been empty, Kate. Numb from Jesse's death, and tired. So *damn* tired. I keep thinking that there's got to be more to life...."

She touched his chest and he felt the tremble of her fingers. He knew he ought to draw back. He had vowed to keep his distance. Frank stepped aside.

Frustration settled in her eyes. It matched his own. "I'm sorry," she said quietly. "That day in the garage... I just assumed—"

"If there are apologies to be made, they're mine. I came to Newton's Crossing, disrupted your life, pulled your son away from his homework more evenings than I care to admit."

"It was my... invitation," she said. She lifted her eyes to his, and though she colored, she did not look away.

"I'm sorry, Kate, not just for what I've done, but for what I can't seem to control. It's late. I'll—"

She was in his arms then and he was kissing her, tasting her mouth in slow motion, stroking her lips with his own in moves meant to caress, not control.

She answered his kiss, moving within the circle of his arms, her every breath matching his, slow, deep, with a quietness that settled into his bones.

"All my life I've lived with men who took what they wanted," he whispered, his voice ragged. "I've been that way, too. Teach me to go slowly, Kate. Show me there's hope, after all."

His heart beat strong and hard, measuring the moments. This was the beginning. He would make it last.

He kissed her again and again, till he couldn't tell where his kiss ended and hers began, until he thought his heart would burst with wanting her, until he knew that she wanted him, knew that she would welcome his touch... once it was time... once he was sure that he could control that wild streak of madness that came out of nowhere, that might interfere....

And then he walked her up the hill, said good-night and left her, before the doubt dared take hold.

* * *

"So, what do you think?" Bobby swung himself around the center post in his loft playroom.

"I think it's high time that you talked to your mother again about the derby car."

"Yeah, maybe. It's getting pretty close to the sign-up deadline. But I know what Mom's going to say. It's all because they're having the race on Rock Top Mountain where my dad got killed. He used to fly down when me and Mom were visiting Grandpop. He'd swoop real low till we ran out and waved. She laughed at first, but when he kept it up she'd get *so* mad...." Bobby crossed the room and reached for a framed photograph on top of his desk.

"This is my dad," Bobby said, staring at the picture intently. "I look like him some. Mom says so. I don't know, I don't remember too good." He handed the picture to Frank. "What do you think?"

Frank thought of his own father, tall, thin, rugged as an Indiana winter till the alcohol broke him. "I think you look like your dad," Frank said, carefully replacing the portrait. "And some like your mother, too. But by and large I'd say that you're your own man, kid."

Bobby grinned and took another spin around the pole. "I'm gonna tell Mom that. I'm gonna tell her she doesn't have to worry about me all the time. But first I'm going to finish the derby car. Promise not to say anything till then?"

"If she asks me about it I can't lie, but I won't bring it up on my own."

"It's going to be a really neat car, Frank."

"No comment, okay? The less I know, the better for both of us."

"The less you know about what, Frank Vincenti?"

The top of Kate's head was all that showed in the loft trapdoor as she swung it open. Frank reached down to give her a hand up the rest of the ladder. Cool and smooth, the touch of her palm made him want to lift her into his arms then and there. He'd wanted to do it since he'd climbed the hill to the house for Sunday dinner. He'd wanted to do it all week, especially since Thursday night, when they'd said with those kisses what neither of them had had much luck saying with words.

I don't know where we're going, but I don't want to turn back.

But there were still things he had to sort out, things he'd pushed to the back of his mind while he'd worked through the weekend on the steady stream of oil leaks and mufflers, flat tires and engines he'd have sworn had not been touched in years.

And the canary yellow hot rod still sat in the second bay. The first part hadn't fit and the second had come in too late Saturday. Maybe this evening—

"The less you know about what?" Kate asked again.

"Mom, Frank says he doesn't know much about school stuff, but he sure does know about math. I did real good on Friday's test."

"You're hiding something, Bobby. You're terrible at that, you know. Is your homework getting sloppy again?"

"Just *trust* me, Mom, okay?"

She touched a corner of his collar. "How can I refuse such a grown-up request?" Then Kate glanced up at Frank. "Whatever your secret is, Bobby, it's in very good hands."

Bobby swung around the post again and grinned at both of them.

"I could use some help down there," Kate said. "I have to change, and we need another place set at the table. Trav just pulled in."

That was one of the customs surrounding Sunday dinner at Newton's Crossing, Frank discovered. People dropped in.

Another was that the women wore dresses. Mattie came in a bright pink tie-dyed skirt and top, with matching ribbons braided into her hair. Kate wore sandals and a gauzy white dress cinched at the waist with a wide turquoise belt. The hem of the skirt swept her calves. She had the most perfectly shaped calves and ankles he'd ever seen on a woman, Frank decided. She'd been hiding them under those jeans that he had once, not that long ago, nearly taken off her....

He stared at her all through dinner, till Trav made some sort of casual remark that he didn't even hear, and Kate's cheeks turned as pink as Mattie's dress. Everyone looked at him and laughed, even Bobby.

But Frank didn't care. Whatever they'd said had included his name in the same breath with hers. Nothing else mattered.

When Kate filled Frank's plate for the third time, Bobby's eyes widened. "Guess you don't eat turkey much, huh, Frank?"

He grinned at the boy. "Not around a table set with silver, candles, napkins made of cloth. There wouldn't have been room between the stacks of automotive manuals.''

Everybody laughed. Under the table, Bobby's dog shifted and rested her head on Frank's boot.

They hadn't changed the welcome sign when Kate's father died, Bobby had explained, nor when Charlie Prescott had moved them away. Lady could count as number five on the sign at the edge of town till somebody else came along, they'd decided. Bobby had looked at him wistfully, Frank remembered, the same way he was looking at him now.

''After the six months is up, are you going to stay?'' the boy asked bluntly.

Bo coughed, Mattie dropped her fork and Kate stood up to clear the table. Each of them in their own way was trying to make it unnecessary for him to answer, he knew. But he wanted to answer. He didn't know what he would say, but—

The shrill sound of a buzzer echoed from the porch. Bobby jumped up. ''I'll go, Mom. I can handle the gas pumps. Just save me some pumpkin pie.''

''I'll go along with the boy,'' Trav said. ''Thanks for the meal, Katie, love. You do your old man proud.'' Trav brushed a whiskered kiss across Kate's cheek, then headed for the door.

She *did* do her father proud, Frank thought. And she'd keep right on doing it. The crossing was always going to be the kind of place where there'd be an extra chair at the Sunday dinner table for anyone passing through.

She met his eyes across the table. Bo and Mattie were stacking dishes and didn't notice. *I'll give you an answer,* he silently promised. And it would be soon, perhaps sooner than either of them expected.

The old red gas pumps glowed a shade deeper in the fading light, and the sky was painted a matching crimson. It washed a subtle pink glow over the front of the garage, the string of vacant buildings on down, even the café and its row of motel rooms out back. Frank saw the logic of Bo's color preference and smiled.

Beyond, at the rear corner of the garage, the lacy green boughs of a paloverde tree hung motionless over the side of Bo and Mattie's empty trailer. They'd gone to the movie with Kate and Bobby.

He crossed to the edge of the road and looked down it. Empty, as far as the eye could see, and silent, a deep, abiding silence that was anything but lonely. At a distant rumble, a whistle of air and the grating echo of a gearshift, Frank turned his back to the sunset and looked east.

A shimmer of silver dotted the horizon. It hovered, then grew larger. Rough and heavy, the noise of the working engine was not close at all to the high-powered whine of the race car. But for a moment Frank remembered the low-riding streak of liquid silver that had ruled his life.

He strode out to the bays, flipped the latch on the hot rod and lifted the hood. He picked up a wrench, tinkered for a while, then laid it down. It was stuffy inside the garage. He crossed to the big bay doors and pushed them open.

The sunset had peaked to a brilliant red orange. The color shot through him, hot, unsettling. The semi had passed without stopping. It labored up the mountain. Frank almost smelled hot rubber, imagined the wide smooth tires, felt the edge of impossible speed.

Then he thought of Kate and stilled.

Back in the office, he dialed his lawyer's Long Beach hotel. "How did it go?"

"First place! Thought you didn't care."

Frank surveyed the garage and thought about all the sale would provide. "I don't care, not in the way you think. Any bids for the Silver Falcon, the racing operation?"

A low chuckle sang over the wire. "They're beating down the doors. The best offer—"

"Spare me the details. Just work it out."

"You really are serious. You aren't coming back."

"There's no way on God's earth I'd consider doing that."

Chapter Eight

Frank was scrubbing up when he heard the truck pull into the crossing. Laughter, a tumble of voices, then a moment later Kate stepped through the open bay door. She didn't even wait till he'd dried his hands to slip into the circle of his arms.

"It's still Sunday," she said. "If I had thought you'd work I'd have *made* you come to the movie."

He kissed a salty corner of her mouth. "You taste like popcorn. What did you see?"

"Disney. Something about dogs."

"Sorry I missed it."

Kate laughed, her breath warm against the open collar of his shirt. "I might have known from the way you treat Lady."

"Dogs, cats, babies, you name it."

"Babies? I never would have guessed."

"You think I don't know about babies? Just because I tinker with cars? Listen, lady, I know about shots and diapers and that stuff you rub on their gums when their teeth are coming in. Jesse was a handful...." He pulled away, knowing he'd said too much. And what did it matter that he'd known how to care for Jesse as a baby, given what had followed?

Then her arms were around him again, more firmly than before. The memories slipped back into perspective. The pain eased.

Her touch was gentle, inviting. He slid his hands up her back, over her shoulders to where the gauzy material of her dress ended, up to the warm soft nape of her neck. He cradled her head and drew it back, kissed her behind her left ear, then began the journey to her mouth.

Kate wriggled away. "If you kiss me again, I'll never get you out of this garage. Come over to the café. I'll put on a pot of coffee."

He grinned, then hesitated and glanced toward the hot rod.

Kate groaned. "Do you really want to go on working?"

"That's the last thing I want. But that car goes home in the morning. It needs a test drive."

"Then do it now or you'll wake everyone up at midnight. I *know you,* Frank Vincenti. If there's the least little thing that doesn't sound right, you'll still be out here when I open the Saguaro in the morning."

"Go with me," he said on impulse. "Send Mattie up to stay with Bobby."

"He's over at the trailer with Bo, working on that derby car, most likely. He thinks I don't know—"

"Then there's no reason not to come."

There was *every* reason not to go, Kate thought moments later, but reason was not what mattered. Trusting her instincts, taking things a day at a time, trusting Frank, that was what counted.

As they sped down the highway, the convertible top down, a rush of air whipped hard around the windshield and caught her braid. Kate moved to get out of the wind. Frank's arm slipped over her shoulder.

Kate laughed. Once she started, she couldn't stop.

"Want to let me in on the joke?"

"I feel like a teenager. It's silly, but—"

"Let's go someplace and make out," he said in a gravelly voice.

Kate whooped and punched him on the thigh. "What a thing to say the first time you take a lady out."

He laughed at that, and then he was quiet. Kate rested her head on his shoulder.

The air stirred up by the moving car was fragrant with the clean scent of her hair and something else, something sweet. The smell grew stronger, and the laughter inside him eased into a feeling he couldn't define. Except that he knew that in some crazy way this *was* the first time he'd taken a woman "out," and what she'd said back at the garage had been strangely true. She did know him, everything about him that was important, anyway.

Beside him, Kate shifted. "Are you happy with your work on the hot rod? Or do you hear some small noise that isn't quite right, feel some errant vibration? Tell me, Frank, are you going to be up all night with this little toy?"

"Try it yourself. Put your hands on the wheel and tell me what you feel."

She grasped the steering wheel and he covered her hands with his. "I'll let go for a moment," Frank said. "Keep your eyes on the center line."

He accelerated slightly. "Feel that?"

"Feel what?"

Her leg had trembled against his thigh. He glanced at her. Kate's lips were parted, concentrating.

"Am I doing okay?" she asked.

He chuckled. "You're doing just fine." He accelerated and covered her hands again with his, and the little car seemed to fly down the road.

Frank could see the angle of the turn ahead clearly in the light of the rising moon. He could judge the bank and the temperature of the asphalt. He knew exactly what speed would be safe yet provide a true test of the work that he'd done. Frank eased the gas pedal down, then down again.

"*Now* do you feel it?"

"Sorry, I don't feel a thing."

"Right!" Frank shouted over the noise of the engine. "No shimmy. No pull. Just a good steady grip on the road with RPMs to spare."

"I'm not much for speed. I never have—"

A siren wailed. Blue lights swung out of a side road then flashed behind them, bouncing off the rearview mirror.

Frank groaned. "Where the hell did he come from?"

"It's Mac. He's been known to sit in that spot all night."

Frank pulled the car off onto the shoulder and waited, and Kate slid back across the seat.

MacMillan got out of the patrol car, ambled toward them, then leaned against the side of the car. "You don't need to show me the registration, Vincenti. I know who owns this car. I've got you for exceeding the safe speed limit on a turn and crossing over the center line."

"Oh, come on, Mac. We were just—"

"The state of Nevada doesn't much care for excuses, Kate." To Frank he said, "I'd like you to get out of your car and come back to the cruiser while I write up the ticket."

A moment later Mac slid into the front seat of his car, switched off the two-way radio and picked up a clipboard. He wrote for a while, then asked without looking up, "Does she know?"

"Know what?"

"I spend a lot of time in this cruiser. I listen to the news. They profiled your Team Vincenti after racing season opened at Long Beach today."

"It's not my team anymore. I'm out of racing. The operation and everything that goes along with it is up for sale."

"Maybe everything *including* the man who designed the car?"

"I told you, that part of my life is over."

"Maybe you ought to fill Kate in, just the same. Maybe she ought to know that you don't need her charity."

"I never said I did."

"Yes, but you let her go on and think it. Didn't you do that, *Mr. Vincenti?* Didn't you let 'em all think that you were just a drifter down on his luck?"

"Listen, MacMillan—"

"*You* listen to *me*. At the least Kate deserves to know that the guy she's riding with lets other people die in the cars he builds."

For a split second Frank wondered just how much time he'd do if he smashed MacMillan square in the face. "Give me the ticket," he said through clenched teeth. "I'll tell her myself."

"Damn right you will, buddy." Mac tore off the sheet. "Here's a little souvenir of Nevada. You can mail in the payment from Indiana. I'm going down to Vegas for a couple of days of training. When I get back, I want you gone. Test your cars on home turf, Vincenti, not in *my* territory."

The patrol car sped away, and Frank crumpled the ticket in a hard tight ball. But he did not drop it. He'd pay the fine all right, but not from Indiana. He'd promised Kate six months.

He took his time getting back to the hot rod. *Had* he deceived her? He'd always been guarded with women, though never dishonest. He just hadn't wanted to talk about the past, that's all. *I'm not much for speed,* she'd said. But speed for its own sake had never interested him, either.

He swung into the hot rod, shoved the stick in gear and threw gravel as he spun the car around. He glanced at Kate once, to make sure she'd buckled her seat belt, then trained his eyes on the road ahead.

"You *were* speeding," she said.

He nodded, silent.

"Mac's bark is ten times worse than his bite."

"He doesn't need bite, he has a badge and a gun."

"Ev told me that shotgun he used last week wasn't even loaded."

Frank didn't respond. They drove another five miles.

"It's not Mac's rotten attitude, is it?"

"No. Kate, we have to talk." He slowed the hot rod, looking for a place to pull off.

A dirt road came up. "Turn there," she said. "It leads to an old lemon grove just beyond that stand of mesquite trees."

The rutted road crossed a dry wash, then climbed a small hill. Frank pulled up to a rusted iron gate and cut the engine.

Stillness settled, save for the hum of an insect. He let the quiet seep inside. Beyond, a moonlit carpet of trees climbed the rise. Their blossoms could have been a blanket of snow in an Indiana winter, he thought. The tension in his gut eased.

"Smells wonderful," Kate said as she moved across the seat.

Stay where you are, he wanted to tell her. It was going to be hard enough… But he lifted his arm to let her move under it, and she slid in close against his side, nuzzled into his shoulder. The scent grew stronger, wrapping them in a fragrant room with walls of darkness and a ceiling of star shine that seemed to go on forever.

How could he tell her here?

How could he describe the past and the hold that his family and the world of racing had once had on him? The words tangled in his head like so much complex timing circuitry. He knew about timing. It could mean the difference between winning the race or sliding off the wall. You timed the braking, the passing, the pit stops.

Was there something he could do before Mac got back and forced the issue, something he could say that would make it clearer? Maybe if he just kept working hard—

"*You* said we needed to talk."

He'd watched her mouth shape the words. "I . . . don't know where to begin."

Kate leaned close. "Begin at the beginning," she whispered, her lips nearly brushing his.

One kiss. Then he'd tell her. Just one kiss.

But at the first taste of her mouth on his, the decision for what happened after was taken from him quickly and thoroughly. She could make him respond in an instant, and she didn't even have to try.

She opened to his kiss like the lemon tree blossoms must have opened to the cool evening air, like that time in his room after the rain when she'd come to him eagerly, as hungrily as he'd come to her, so hungry that the union of their lips had quickly seemed inadequate.

Her hands joined his in a remembered dance of joy. "Touch me everywhere, Frank," she whispered. She drew his hand to her cheek, to her mouth, down the curve of her throat to the valley of her breasts.

His mouth followed the path of his touch, relearning every curve of her body, every hidden crevice. Kate sighed and reached out, tugging at the buckle of his belt.

He caught her hand then, struggling with himself, but it was too late. Her open palm moved down his body.

His words rasped through clenched teeth. "Kate, Kate, what you do to me. You just don't know—"

She covered his lips with her fingertips and then with her mouth, till he couldn't have spoken if he'd wanted to, except with his body.

He pulled her astride him, pushing aside his clothes and hers till their bodies were free.

And then, they joined. It was like coming home—familiar, because they'd almost been together once before; right, because he knew she wanted him just as much as he wanted her.

Moonlight fell on her lowered lashes. Lips parted, she whispered his name, over and over. Frank closed his own eyes as the music of her voice filled his head, pushing every thought toward oblivion.

She moved against him then, gaining control. She was straddling him, her knees against the seat of the car. She moved again, hesitated, and moved once more.

He tensed to hold back. He wanted to be careful, to protect her, to love her as she deserved. *"Kate."*

She kissed away the ragged sound of her name on his lips, easing his struggle to speak with her need for silence. But all the while she moved against him, slowly, then quickly, then slowly again, drawing him closer and closer toward the edge.

And then suddenly his mouth broke free. His hands slid to her waist. With one smooth motion he lifted her up, then down across the seat.

He did not hesitate as he pushed her legs apart with his knees. He didn't stop to ask if she could take the full weight of his body. He didn't speak. He didn't think. He just became what he was, a man with a hell-bent passion, pursuing the woman who embodied it.

The miracle was, she matched him. Matched the power of his thrust with the rising grind of her hips, matched the force of kiss till he wasn't sure if the blood he tasted was hers or his own, matched the reckless pounding of his body buried in hers without inhibition, without restraint.

Then suddenly his power gathered and burst into one final thrust that ended in sweet release. Kate cried out then, too, and in one long shudder of ecstasy, she joined him.

For a moment he did not know where he was, save enveloped in the spell of the flowers and of their love-making, the brilliance of the stars, the silence. Finally she spoke.

"I won't break," she whispered, as though discovering it for herself. He rose on his forearms to look at her. "You don't have to be careful, Frank. It's all right. That was it, wasn't it... that night on the porch?"

He was too full to speak, of the star-studded night, of something new and old, exotic and simple all wrapped into one incommunicable feeling. Yet, she seemed to know, seemed to understand.

"It's *very* all right," he said finally. "It's going to be all right from now on out."

For a long time they simply held each other.

Later they talked, about life at the crossing, life in general. For the first time she told him the whole story of her life with Charles Prescott, about how she'd met and married quickly—too quickly, she'd said, to be sure they were matched.

"Charlie didn't change," she said in thoughtful summation. "He just *became* more completely himself."

Frank nodded, thoughtful, and wondered how long it would take him to become the new self he envisioned.

"I tried never to stand in his way," she said.

"I'm sure you succeeded. You're very good at that, at letting people . . . be."

He found himself saying things to her that he'd never said to anyone. He talked to her about raising Jesse, about the crazy things they'd done when they were kids, about innumerable details he'd forgotten. It all came flooding back, all the good things he'd had with his kid brother.

And that led him to talk about what he believed, about trust, generosity, loyalty, things he saw in her, things he'd striven all his life to make a part of himself.

Finally he drove her back to the crossing, put the hot rod away in the garage, then walked her up the hill.

They stood outside on the porch looking down at the crossroads, arms entwined, her back to his chest. Mattie came out but Kate didn't move away.

"High time you two got together," Mattie said, then hurried on down the hill.

Then Kate turned and they shared kisses, languid with the surety of lovers who know that there will be other nights, other embraces.

"It's late," she finally whispered against his lips. "Tomorrow's Monday."

Reluctantly he eased his embrace. "Kate, there's so much more that I need to tell you."

"Tell me tomorrow," she said. "Tomorrow will be soon enough."

She kissed him again and slipped inside. He turned and headed down the path.

He should have told her before they'd made love, Frank thought. But he hadn't known it was going to happen...no, he *had* known. He'd known since the day he'd turned back with Bobby, since the morning he'd told Mac that he'd be staying on to take care of things. He had known the first time he saw her. He'd known even though he'd fooled himself into believing that the whole thing was temporary, a short stay in a place quiet enough to let his heart heal.

But he had not known that it could be like this. Rough, abandoned, out-of-mind passion. Wild and intoxicating like the liquor he never touched, addictive like the cocaine he'd heard about. Only better by far because it lasted. It left him feeling full of more than just physical warmth. It left him full of wanting and needing more and believing that something, someone, *Kate,* could touch that dark place in his soul where he'd never dared look.

He'd lost control. Frank shook with the thought of it. But Kate had matched him.

He found himself standing in front of his room. He put his key into the lock and turned it. Up on the hillside the light still shone from her front porch. He watched it flicker, then go out.

He couldn't sleep. The hours passed. Midnight came and went. He'd begun to rehearse how he would tell her. *I used to own a racing team. I built cars that went very fast. In an indirect way, I caused the death of my brother.*

His ties to his family had died with Jesse. Why couldn't the past die, too? He'd kept quiet about it, partly to ensure that people like Mac who could never believe he'd leave racing wouldn't get in the way of his doing it.

But that had been needless. Nothing could make him go back now.

On Monday morning Kate woke to a sweep of fragrant fresh air. A glass on the sill beneath the open window held the spray of blossoms that Frank had insisted on picking.

He'd wanted to fill her lap with them.

Laughter bubbled up inside her at the memory, then something quieter and deeper. She imagined lying with him, somewhere out in the open, her body covered with blossoms as Frank's warm breath blew them away one by one.

She had loved his touch, both the gentle and the not-so-gentle strokes. And when he'd taken her with reckless disregard for anything but the depth of his passion, she'd learned something new about herself.

It was safe to let go, safe in a way that it had never been with Charlie. She wasn't sure why. She only knew that given time Frank would stop treating her as though she were fragile, and she, in turn, would recapture something of herself she'd lost with Charlie's death, maybe long before. Given even a month with half again as many nights, there'd be no fragility left between them, only the strong silent bond that holds two people who have plumbed each other's limits.

Please, God, she prayed. Just let there be time enough.

Kate wrote Bobby a hasty note about numerous neglected chores and the golden opportunity he had to catch up during the three day vacation for teacher training at school. Then she slipped out of the house and headed down the hill.

Kate went about opening the café, trying to concentrate on her usual list of concerns. But all of them vanished when Frank came in, shortly after Bo and Mattie.

He pushed through the Saguaro's front screen door, his eyes flashing silver, his dark hair damp and curly from a shower. He looked even taller, Kate thought, as though some weight had been lifted off his shoulders. And she, in turn, felt light as air.

He strode across the floor, thumped Bo on the back, gave Mattie an uncharacteristic kiss on the cheek, then turned to Kate. And then, right there in front of the crew and five or six truckers, he lifted Kate off her feet and swung her around and around.

"I'm hungry as hell, woman. What have you got for breakfast?"

"It's a café, Frank," she said through her laughter. "You can order anything you want."

"What I *want* is to shut this place down and take you for a ride—"

"No *way*," boomed Trav. "Us truckers would starve."

"And you've got cars waiting at the garage," Mattie added.

"You got time to eat," Bo said. "We got fresh strawberries. Trav's buddy from L.A. just brought 'em in."

Kate glanced outside at the big blue rig parked beside Trav's silver one, and across the street at the three cars parked in front of the garage. "Hurry up with those pancakes, Bo," she said as she poured Frank's coffee.

"Ain't nothin' them fancy places got that the crossing can't match," Bo said. "Two darn pretty women, good food, fresh air and one hell of a place to get your car fixed. Only a fool would ask for more."

Minutes later, as she walked him to the door, Frank was insistent. "Tonight we talk. No diversions, no interruptions. There are things about me that you need to know."

"I know the important things already."

"Maybe," he said. "I hope so." She followed him outside, teasing that he had no right to make her wait all day.

In the middle of the street she stopped, eyes wide. "You're not with the mob?"

He roared with laughter. "You've seen too many movies. It's nothing like that, and unless you follow sports—"

His words were cut off as a late-model pickup pulled up alongside them. "You done with m' boy's car yet, son?"

Frank caught Kate's eye. She knew what he wanted to say. She wanted to say it, too. *We'd like to keep the hot rod another day, another night, maybe even make you an offer.*

"Tonight?" he called after her as she turned back to the café.

"Of course," she answered.

What more could there be to say if they did talk later? She'd heard that the life of an athlete could be hard. Road trips from city to city, motel rooms and restaurants not half as good as the Saguaro Café. No wonder he was tired of the life.

And what had his game been? He was tall enough for basketball, but somehow the image didn't fit. Maybe football? He did have the measure of killer instinct that she'd always imagined was needed on the gridiron. But, no, if she had to guess, she'd pick baseball. She thought of Frank's natural aloofness, his sense of control, of the easy way he moved his body. She thought of his hands, the way he'd tossed Bobby's ball to her that first night on the porch.

It had to be baseball, Kate thought as she headed for the café. And what would Bobby have to say, once he learned that the tall, quiet man who'd been pitching to him lately had once been a star? It would be proof right there that the crossing wasn't dull. A little isolated sometimes, maybe, but never, never dull.

Back in the café, every stool at the counter and every table was occupied. Mattie shot Kate a harried look and waved toward the backed-up orders over Bo's grill. Kate grabbed a tray and started loading it.

"Hey, Kate," Trav called out. "You've got to see—"

"Be there in a minute," she said.

Trav and his trucker friend were poring over the newspaper when she finally got back to the rear table. Bobby was hopping from side to side, trying to see over their shoulders.

"You wouldn't believe how business has picked up since Frank and Bo opened the garage again," Kate said as she filled Trav's cup, then the trucker's.

"Sure is a friendly place," the man said, "now that your cook's got something else to do besides fuss at his wife."

Trav tapped the newspaper spread out on the table. "If you think Newton's Crossing is busy now, just wait."

Kate glanced at the feature article with its flashy pictures. Everything about the car spelled motion—the sleek silver line of the aerodynamic body, the huge black tires, the sweeping royal blue stripes on the front and back fins and along the side. *Race cars*. Just what Bobby *didn't* need to be reading about.

"Frank's far too humble for his own good," Trav said.

"He gave me tips," Bobby said proudly. "He told me about fixing my derby car's design. That silver car, Mom, look at it!" Bobby bounced up and down in his chair. "Did you ever see anything so sharp? And guess what, Mom? You'll never guess—"

"Bobby, calm down. You're going to spill Trav's coffee."

"Mom, *that's Frank's car*."

Time stopped. The fly inching up the outside of the plate glass window reached the crack and halted. The jukebox clicked off. At the grill, Bo turned slowly, spatula raised, his mouth opening as if to speak. It all seemed to take an eternity.

Then Bobby's elbow tipped over the salt and scattered it across the table. A song began to play. Bo said, "Kate..."

"Mom, did you hear me? Frank *owns* this race car."

Her voice sounded strange to her, an echo from far away. "I heard you, Bobby. And who owns the wrecked car? Does Frank own that one, too?"

Trav bent over the paper to read the caption. "That's the accident twelve years ago that killed Al Vincenti, Frank's father."

"He was founder of Vincenti Racing," the trucker said. "It's all right here, all about the family and the way Frank took over when his father died. Frank was about to get his big break when his brother took his car out and wrecked it. The car caught fire..."

It was all she could do to mumble that she knew about Frank's brother's death, knew that he'd died in a car wreck recently. But even as she spoke she saw the flames lick the race car, and Frank's arm.

"Guess he's had a hard time," Trav was saying. "It's no wonder he wanted to get away for a while. And he couldn't have chosen a better place."

"He didn't really choose the crossing," Kate managed to say. "He just happened through." *We chose him.*

"Still, he's done a lot at the crossing since he came," Trav said. He winked at Bobby. "Guess that derby car design is in great shape."

Bobby groaned. "Mom, please don't be mad. I didn't mean to keep it so quiet. You're just so weird about that mountain. I figured when you saw the car—''

She hushed him with a touch to his shoulder. "We'll talk about it later, Bobby. Finish up your breakfast, now. Then you'd better take care of Lady."

"That's another thing Frank did for us," Bobby was saying as she walked away. "He helped me fix this thing I invented for my dog."

In the dish room, Kate leaned against the wall and covered her ears. She didn't want to hear a single more detail about how Frank had come so quietly, so unassumingly into their lives, about how he had reconciled Mattie and Bo, brought the garage to life, done one thing after another to win Bobby's admiration. Her throat burned with tears that would not rise.

He'd said he would stay six months. Perhaps he'd thought that it would take that long to get over his brother's death. He would leave when the time was up. Why would a race car driver want to stay in a little dust bowl of a town out West?

What would they do then, she and Bobby, Mattie and Bo, and all the people who were so happy that the garage had opened again? What would they do if he left?

And what would she *do if he stayed?*

Words from the past broke in, her mother's whispered words from a lifetime ago. *I never tried to change your dad, Katie. Don't try to change the man you marry. A man's got to be allowed to be himself.* Oh, she'd learned that lesson very well.

She thought of Pop, happy all his sixty-eight years in grease up to his elbows night and day, and of Charlie, himself to the fiery, bitter end, and she thought of the warnings she'd bitten back, first to Pop, then to her own husband. She'd tried her best not to make Charlie feel guilty about the path he had chosen. As she'd told Frank, she'd never said a word. She had been accepting, all right. Or maybe she'd just put up a good front.

She'd been like ice in bed. She couldn't love a man and risk losing him, so she'd loved less, and without even realizing it.

Till Frank.

Kate looked down at her hands. Tears had pooled in her open palms. She wiped them on her apron.

She wouldn't cry anymore. She would go across to the garage, find Frank and tell him she'd changed her mind, tell him the garage was not for rent, that she was thinking of moving out as Ev had suggested. She'd tell him something, *anything*. Just to make him go.

Chapter Nine

"My grandson's got to get into Summit City to work or he'll move off the property," the elderly rancher told Frank. "Fix up the truck. I'll pay little by little if that's okay by you."

"No problem," Frank said.

He'd heard the same thing all last week. He'd written the estimates as inexpensively as he could, then agreed to float the charges. Fifty percent of the customers were going to be paying until Christmas.

"Parts store in Summit City ain't going to be so understanding," Bo said when he did the books. When he'd gotten to the lady who was paying in produce and eggs, Bo had nearly died laughing. "You sure ain't no businessman, Frank."

But the café could use everything the woman delivered, and he couldn't turn these people away just because they didn't have ready cash. Besides, now that the racing operation had sold he had plenty of seed money to get the garage back on its feet.

He helped the rancher and his grandson unhitch the truck and push it into the bay. When he turned around, he saw Kate.

She was standing across the road in the long shadow cast by the cactus sign, looking up toward Rock Top Mountain. Frank knew immediately that something was wrong.

It seemed to take forever—the grandson's awkward attempts to express appreciation, the handshakes, the agreement on a pickup date. When they finally pulled away, in a truck as dilapidated as the one they'd left for him to repair, Frank headed across the road.

She took a few steps toward him, then stopped. For a moment Frank thought she was going to turn away. "Kate, what is it?"

"I...Trav's friend from the coast brought the *L.A. Times,*" she said. "There's an article about your family, about...what you do for a living."

"Kate..."

She looked up at him, her eyes a bright, glassy green. "I understand why you had to get away from Indianapolis."

"Kate, I never meant to deceive you. I just wanted to forget—"

"But I told you, I understand. To lose your father, and then your only brother like that, it must have been horrible."

He wanted to tell her that it was so much more than just losing Jesse.

"I've got to get back to the café, Frank."

"Mattie's on with Bo. Come across the street to the garage."

"But I told you, there's no need. I understand."

"You *don't* understand. How could you? I hardly understand it myself."

She was standing right next to him, but she might as well have been in China, and his impatient tone seemed to push her even further away. "Please," he said more gently. "Come across to the garage."

Once inside, he could see her fear gathering, spilling into anger. He closed the office door, wanting to bolt it to keep her from running.

"Sit down," he said. It came out sounding like an order.

Kate remained standing. He gestured toward the chair. She ignored it.

"It's quite a car. Bobby was impressed. I'm sure my son will have lots of new ideas for the derby car that you're helping him build."

"I'm glad he told you about the car."

"He told Trav. I haven't talked to Bobby about the soap box derby since the day he first brought it up."

"It's a simple gravity car, Kate. There isn't even an engine."

"I just think there are better things that Bobby could be doing with his time. Ev White says—"

"She's got some crazy idea that third-grade arithmetic ought to be dosed out like foul-tasting medicine."

"I've known Ev since we were kids in school ourselves. She's tough on Bobby because she cares about him."

"Maybe she cares too much. Does she treat all the kids the way she treats him? Here every day, hovering like a hen."

"You're exaggerating."

"You're closing your eyes."

"I just *don't* want my son on Rock Top Mountain. It was a hard time for him, losing his father like that. He doesn't need to be reminded."

"*You* don't need to be reminded," Frank said gently.

She shook her head. "Mattie's the superstitious one. The fact that my husband was killed on that mountain doesn't make it unlucky."

"Then why don't you want Bobby in the race?"

"I don't want him working on cars."

"Your father was a mechanic. All I've heard since I got here is what a genius he was. Just because a man works with his hands—"

"It's not that. I don't want Bobby fooling with things that might lead to... he has mechanical inclinations. He gets that from his father."

"Kate, look at me."

She refused to lift her eyes.

Frank reached out and tipped her chin, forcing her gaze even with his. "Just because Bobby builds model airplanes, or other things with wheels, doesn't mean he's going to test jets someday, Kate."

"But look at your own life. Can you honestly say that your father's involvement with race cars had nothing to do with the path that you and your brother chose?"

He flinched, then laughed, the sound of it brittle. "It pushed me in the other direction. At MIT I specialized in automobile safety designs, the kind of features that would compensate for the hotheaded streak that runs in my family. When I finished college I went to Detroit, not back to my father's racing shop.''

''You changed your mind.''

''My father died. I felt responsible for Jesse.''

''But you ended up in racing.''

''Jesse's dead. I'm free to do anything now.''

Kate glanced at the bays and the rusty old truck in the middle of the clean-swept floor. He knew she was seeing the sleek silver car.

''You'll go back,'' she said quietly.

''No.''

''Before a test, Charlie breathed rarefied air. Afterward, he'd talk for days about what a thrill it had been. Bobby was only four, but he listened, rapt. Then Charlie would wear down, mention quitting. Once he even called a real estate agent to see about selling the Lancaster house, but he forgot all about it by the next week's test.''

''I'm not Charles Prescott, Kate.''

''No. Well . . . it's a beautiful car,'' Kate said. ''It's not that hard to imagine the thrill you must get when you drive it. The article called it the Silver Falcon. It made me think of the tattoo—''

Frank stood abruptly and caught her shoulders. ''Kate, *listen* to me. I don't drive. I built the car, oversaw the tests, modified the designs. I did a million things on the Falcon, but I never raced it.''

''But that night on the porch . . . you said you were your father's son.''

He began to pace. ''I'm still a Vincenti. There's a part of me that's tied to my family, an out-of-control part I'm trying to change, but it doesn't have anything to do with racing."

"Then even if you did go back—"

"I'm *never* going back. The car, the equipment, the semi that hauls it, all of it has been *sold*, Kate. My lawyer called with the news this morning."

He could see that she wanted to believe him. He tried to tell her with his eyes, tried to make her see that he wasn't the happy-go-lucky fly-boy she'd met one lighthearted summer, the man who'd leaped at the first opportunity to take on a life of risk, even when it meant leaving a young son fatherless, his wife a widow.

"When I make a commitment I keep it. I said six months. Do we still have a deal?"

She looked away, confused. "Maybe the past is part of who we are. Maybe we can't get rid of it, even when we want to. I used to think I married Charlie because he seemed my opposite, funny where I was serious, changeable where I was steady. Now I think maybe I married him because of something else, something in me that I don't want to know about. I don't know. I don't know *you*. I'm not even sure that I know myself."

"Give me six months, Kate. *Do* we still have a deal?"

"After race cars I should think you'd be looking for something a little more challenging."

"Have you talked to Bo lately? Has he given you any idea what it's going to take to keep the cars around here on the road? Take that truck, for instance. *Talk* about challenge..."

"If that's the kind of challenge you're looking for, the lift in the garage is operating on borrowed time. There's another temperamental cooler on top of the motel units, and we've even got a well that runs dry occasionally long about September. The crossing won't let you down."

He leaned forward across the desk and took her hands. He wanted to go on holding them forever, as though in doing that they could keep anything from coming between them—his past, hers, an uncertain future.

"I am quite certain that Newton's Crossing, and you, won't ever let me down, Kate."

She lowered her eyes and gently withdrew her hands from his. "I'd better get back. Bobby's home and fit to be tied because school's out for three days, and he wanted to take in the news article about the race, un- less—"

"No thanks. My lawyer gave me the basics. I don't care about the rest."

She nodded, already starting for the door. He wanted to follow, hold her, make sure that she really did understand.

Kate smiled at him, distantly, he thought, but maybe it was just the light.

Back at the café, Bobby shoved his math paper into Kate's hands. "I did my homework first, just like you said, Mom. Can I go back to the trailer and work on my derby car design? Bo says we can start building tomorrow. I bet Frank will want to help. We're going to use silver paint, Mom, just like Frank's race car."

The cook grabbed the swatter and waved it in pursuit of an imaginary fly, while Mattie kept running a cloth across the same patch of counter. Kate wanted to lecture them both about keeping secrets.

But Bobby had needed their support at a time when she'd been unable to give it. She was grateful they'd been there for him. And his race would come and then be over. Maybe by then she'd get used to the idea that her son had no fear at all of Rock Top Mountain, even though the memory still haunted her dreams.

"Mom, can I go?"

Kate glanced at the paper. "These numbers aren't the neatest and you'll have plenty of time tomorrow—"

"Aw, Mom."

"Go on then. I'll see you at lunch."

"Thanks, Mom. And thanks for understanding about the derby car."

Bobby's quick, hard hug caught Kate off guard. A wave of the old easy comfort of the crossing swept through her. It *was* going to be all right.

At half past noon, Bobby showed up at the garage. He stood in the office doorway, hopping on one foot and then another and grinning ear to ear, waiting while Frank went over charges with an elderly customer.

"Keep your receipt," he told the woman. "The converter is factory warranted. My labor's guaranteed, too."

"You don't have to worry," Bobby piped up. "Frank *builds* cars. They race on the track at Indianapolis and other places, too. He does really good work!"

The woman peered at Frank over the top of her bifocals. "Well, I declare. A race car driver right here in Newton's Crossing."

"No, ma'am. I used to *build* race cars. Others drove them."

"Same thing."

"No, and I'm not in that line of work anymore."

The woman left and before Frank could say anything, the boy was pulling him out the door. "Mom says you've got to eat," he said. "While I'm off from school I'm going to let you know when it's time. *I'm* going to take care of *you*, Frank."

Frank glanced around the garage and thought about all the work he'd get done if he just skipped dinner and counted on Bo to bring him something later. Then the boy tugged his arm again. He looked down into eager green eyes. No contest.

"Come on, kid. I'm hungry as all get-out. Thanks for reminding me."

Kate greeted them both with a gentle touch and a quick smile, too busy for more, Frank knew.

Half an hour later, Bo heaped a second serving of mashed potatoes on a pork chop platter and set it down on the counter. "Man, you put away more food than anybody I ever seen, *when* you remember to eat."

"Guess what?" Bobby announced. "I'm going to put a seat belt in my car. Bo says there's a roll of old webbing out in the trailer. Would you help me, Frank? I want a *real* racing harness like it shows in the picture."

Once again Bobby unfolded the newspaper. Frank glanced at the photo of a group of men strapping a driver into a car, then quickly looked away.

"What do you think, Frank? Could we do it?"

He took his time answering. "Safety's important, but you won't need a harness, kid. The soap box cars aren't that fast."

"I heard that you can get going pretty good. I heard—"

"Bobby, let Frank eat in peace," Kate said. "Have you given Lady that brushing yet?"

Bobby bounded for the door, making a noise like a truck changing gears.

Bo chuckled, then glanced at Kate and quieted.

"I hate to see him get his hopes up, that's all," she said. "I haven't gone over the race rules yet. They say there are several new ones."

"Sounds like they copy big-time racing in more ways than one," Bo said. "I hear it's hell to keep up, huh, Frank?"

"Why would they alter the rules?" Kate asked.

Frank shrugged, wishing they'd change the subject, but all eyes were on him, waiting for an answer. "Safety," he said quietly.

"To a point," Bo added, "but it's mostly money. Racing's got to be exciting or the fans won't turn out or turn on the TV. They've got to manipulate the rules. It's the same darn thing in bike racing. But there's nothing like winning to prove your machine can take punishment. Shoot, I ain't ever known anybody to go to Indy. Man, I'd *love* to drive that car myself."

A plate hit the floor and shattered. Mattie bent to pick up the pieces.

"Lucky for us she wasn't carrying a mirror," Bo joked. "Two years is long enough to wait for your luck to change. Seven would be an eternity."

A trucker at the middle table laughed. "Sure can't imagine you in a race car, Bo. They'd have to build it twice as wide."

The big man looked out the window, his soft eyes dreamy. "I could lose weight."

"Come *on,*" the trucker chided.

Mattie tossed the last of the broken plate pieces into a dishpan. "He loves to watch those races on TV," she told the trucker. "And Kate, you said that about your husband—that his flying career began with just watching."

"Mattie, your superstition is getting out of hand. Bo's no more likely to drive a race car—"

"I know, but he could go back to bike racing. He's fixed up the bike. You don't know what it's like. Someone used to pull alongside and challenge him... he'd just go crazy."

Bo hung his head. "Mattie, I know I promised."

Mattie moved on down the counter without answering. When she got to Frank, she collected his dishes, head bowed.

Frank glanced around the café. His past had entered it like a shadow, clouding the peace and goodwill. "I have to get back to the garage," he muttered.

Bo chuckled. "Back to the basics, huh, Frank?"

"Those *basics* keep families around here on the road for months, Bo. That's worth a hell of a lot more than winning some auto race."

The big man lifted both hands in mock surrender. "Okay, okay, I didn't mean nothin'."

Frank pushed away from the counter and strode toward the door. "Lunch was good. Thanks."

* * *

By suppertime Bobby had all of them climbing the walls. He'd stopped every customer who'd come into the café to brag about Frank's race car, and he'd shown the article so many times its edges were tattered.

He'd peppered Bo with questions about motorbikes and race cars until even the big cook had begged for a break and gone off to his trailer muttering, "That *kid*." But Bobby hadn't bothered Frank. Kate had seen to that.

"Mom?"

"Not yet."

"But Mom—"

"We'll take him a tray in a little while."

"A little while" stretched to nearly nine. Even Kate grew concerned. The light across the street had shone so steadily for so many evenings she'd begun to take it for granted that Frank was just one to work hard. Maybe she'd been wrong to be so accepting.

Bobby had curled up with a book out in the dish room and promptly fallen asleep. When Kate finished readying the tray, she considered slipping out without him. But her son would never forgive her, she knew.

She shook his shoulder gently. "Bobby? It's time."

He yawned and then scrambled to his feet and grabbed a big roll of paper. "It's just something I want to ask Frank about."

"Bobby—"

"Please, Mom. It'll just take a minute. I know he won't mind."

She locked the café and they headed across the street, Kate, Bobby and even Lady, Bobby marching ahead with the roll of paper like a sleepy drum major leading a parade.

They had to thread their way through cars tagged for repair. When they entered the garage they heard music from Pop's old radio and the intermittent sound of the air pump. "Give me just a minute," Frank called out from beneath the truck on the hydraulic lift.

A minute turned into ten before Frank finally switched off the light and joined them in the garage office.

Kate had spread out his dinner on a clean dish towel. Fried chicken, Bo's coleslaw, her own fresh biscuits. He washed, then sank into the old swivel chair.

Bobby pulled up a crate and sat at his elbow. Frank's napkin skidded to the floor and Bobby retrieved it. Frank started to get up to refill his cup with water. "I'll do it," Bobby insisted. He grabbed the cup and headed for the washroom.

Frank lifted an eyebrow. Kate rolled her eyes. "I was right to keep him away. He's driven us crazy all day. He'd have done the same to you, and judging from the cars out front, you're busier than we ever expected."

"It's okay, both the business and the kid."

"I like helping Frank," Bobby said, returning. "I thought maybe tomorrow since I'm off school I could answer the phone, maybe learn to take messages. Bo said a load of parts came in. I could put 'em away."

"You have chores to do up at the house, Bobby. We agreed you'd clean your room, for one thing, and you're to sweep the porch and pull weeds in the garden."

"Your mother's jobs come first, kid. You can come over to the garage in the afternoon, if it's okay with her."

"You don't know what you're in for," Kate said.

He chuckled. "Oh, I think I do. I had a kid brother once who liked to hang out and hand me wrenches."

"I wish I had a brother," Bobby said. "It's not too late, though, huh, Mom? If you got married again..." Bobby's voice trailed off and his eyes slid unabashedly back and forth between them.

Kate felt her face turn crimson. She couldn't speak. And she couldn't look at Frank.

"How's the siphon working on Lady's dish, kid?" At his gentle question the old dog raised her head and sniffed the air.

"It's working real good," Bobby said. "And I've got another idea, too." Bobby smoothed the roll of paper out on the desk and anchored it on the corners with automotive catalogs.

Frank studied the design while Bobby shifted impatiently from one foot to the other. "What do you think? Will it work?"

Frank didn't answer. He reached into the desk drawer and brought out a triangular ruler, measured, wrote, then measured again. "You've drawn to scale?"

"Uh-huh. Do you think—"

"I think you're going to exceed the dimension limits."

"But not by much. It said in the article that *your* new car introduced a lot of changes. It 'pushed the limits,' the writer said. I don't see why—"

"You have to play according to the rules, Bobby."
Frank looked up, across the desk at Kate.

"But maybe they'll change the rules, or give me an exception when they see how good this design is."

"It doesn't work like that, kid. You innovate *inside* the parameters. Then sometimes they change the rules."

"*Darn.* I want my car to look more like yours, Frank. I want it to go *fast*. It says in the article that you've built the fastest car on the Indy circuit. It says in the article—"

"Bobby, that's enough."

"Winning isn't everything, kid."

"But, *Mom.*"

"Your mother's right, Bobby. And I've been meaning to ask you something else. Put the *L.A. Times* piece away, huh? The Silver Falcon's been sold. I'd just as soon forget it."

Bobby swallowed, hard. "Okay, Frank, but I want to take the article to school and show it to all the kids."

Kate stood abruptly. "You've been on the phone all day, Bobby, and on top of every customer who'll listen. When you go back to school, I want you to concentrate on your studies."

Bobby rolled up the paper slowly, every part of his small body drooping. "I don't see why . . . aw, heck, I guess I'll head up to the house."

"He's tired," Kate said. "Too much excitement."

"It will all die down. In a week or two no one will remember."

"Is that what you want?"

"More than anything. And you?"

"I guess I want Bobby to build his car, race it, then go on to other things. He's just a curious little boy. I'm hoping he'll outgrow this *obsession*...."

"Jesse was the same. Sometimes I think I'd have succeeded in heading him in another direction if my father's memory hadn't always been there to pull him back to racing."

"Charlie would have done the same with Bobby."

"Maybe not. Your husband flew the jets himself. If I'd been the one to climb into those cars...maybe my brother might never have had to do it."

His words hung between them, and Kate wanted to gather them up and string them together differently, somehow helping him get to a truth that seemed just beyond reach.

Frank picked up a wrench and headed out to the garage.

"You can't keep working like this."

"Work helps me forget."

"What is it, Frank? What weighs on you so heavily?"

He turned back. "Maybe your husband's love of risky tricks would have freed Bobby. Maybe I could have done the same for Jesse by driving. And maybe if I hadn't stopped at the crossing, if I'd never opened up this garage—"

"That's like saying it's *all* bad. I don't believe that for a moment. Even my marrying Charlie..." She shook her head. Now her own words were confused. Maybe working late would help her, too.

It would have done no good for Bobby to have left the article at home. By noon the next day, the phone lines were jammed and even Frank had given up trying to keep a low profile. The news of his racing background had spread like wildfire.

Business at the garage was booming, Bo told Kate at lunchtime. Even little kids were bringing in their bikes to get air in the tires and steal a quick look at the man who owned an Indy race car. It would get worse day after tomorrow when Bobby went back to school and told everyone he saw.

Each time Bo visited the garage, he stayed a little longer. Finally Kate dug out the names and phone numbers of the college students who'd stopped in looking for work at spring break.

Midafternoon she checked the garage and found Bo up to his elbows in grease on a two-man transmission job. She'd have to go into town for groceries herself, and pay double at the market since the wholesale house would be closed.

"If that ex-Marine who wants to cook calls before I get back, tell him he's hired," she yelled to Mattie on her way out.

Half an hour later in Summit City, she ran into Mac.

"Riding with speeders lately?" he asked as he handed her groceries up into the bed of the truck.

"How was the training, Mac? Learn any new ways to catch those speeders?"

"Oh, come on, Kate, I did what I had to. By the way, I hear your *mechanic* decided to stick around."

"He's taken out a six-month lease on the garage."

"You got that on paper?"

She pressed her lips together and said nothing. As she settled the last of the bags, Mac reached for her hand to help her down. She accepted reluctantly.

"He won't stay, Kate. Ever been to an auto race? All that dust and danger, the sound of the crowd—it hooks you, hard. It'll rub off on Bobby. They're a different breed, Kate. They're not like you and me."

She was about to ask him just how he meant that, but Mac went on. "I've been thinking you're right about gambling being wrong for the crossing, Kate. But maybe there are other things we could do."

"Oh, Mac, I—"

"Come on, Kate, hear me out. Take that dry goods store for example. It's got a lot of empty space, plenty of room for dancing, and good acoustics with that high old ceiling."

"You want to open a dance hall? Bring in liquor, and the crossing would—"

"No, we could do something quieter, more family oriented, square dancing maybe. I'd be willing to sink funds into a mutual project like that. We'd make good partners, you and I."

"Mac, you and I will never in a million years be partners."

"I've got patience, Kate. After Vincenti's been gone awhile—"

"Mac, you're interested in me because I'm out of reach. I always will be. Please, don't ever mention this again."

She headed for the cab, tossed her purse onto the seat and climbed in beside it. She threw the truck in gear, then leaned out the window. "Come out to the crossing, Mac. Frank's committed to the garage. See for yourself. Bring Ev.''

MacMillan colored and scuffed one boot.

But later that evening, near closing time, Mac did come, and he had Ev White with him. Bobby's teacher wore a new red dress with white polka dots and a halter top. Its full skirt billowed when she hopped out of the patrol car. Even the new cook did a double take when Ev walked in the Saguaro's front door.

"What on *earth* have you done to your hair?" Mattie said.

Ev's chin shot out as she pushed back the frizzy curls. "I got a perm in Las Vegas. I don't know why I never tried one before."

"I think it's real becoming," Kate said.

"Wonder what else she got in Vegas?" Mattie mumbled.

Kate shot Mattie a warning frown and grabbed a tub to clear the remaining tables.

"Where's Bobby?" Ev asked, returning. "Has he got that spring project done yet? I don't suppose you've had time to take him to the library."

"He's out behind the trailer with Bo."

"Working on that silly car, I suppose. I don't know why he's bothering now. The sign-up deadline passed this afternoon. I'm glad you came to your senses, Kate. You can't let all this race car talk—"

Kate tore off her apron, pushed by Ev and out the back door, running up the path, taking the railroad-tie steps two at a time.

At her desk she rummaged till she found the papers. She read them quickly and reached for a pen.

The front screen door flew open. "Mom!"

Bobby's tear-streaked face was peppered with sawdust, and his small fits were clinched at his sides.

Kate scrawled her signature. ''We're going for a ride. Just as soon as I—''

''It's too late, Mom. Miss White says the deadline's passed. I thought maybe if I didn't bug you about it all the time, you'd go ahead and sign.''

Bobby flew out the door. Kate grabbed her purse, stuffed the papers inside and followed.

Chapter Ten

Frank stepped out of his room into dry desert air and the violet light of early evening. Ten minutes in the shower had washed away all traces of the grueling day, even the nagging feeling that he ought to have stuck around and knocked out a few more orders. But tonight was his own, and Kate's.

Then halfway across the parking lot he met the trooper. "Planning to fix some more cars before you head out, Vincenti? One of them *won't* be Ev's. Your prices are steep. Folks around here can't afford frills."

Frank nodded and kept on walking toward the café.

MacMillan blocked his path. "Kate says you're in for six months. What about after that?"

"Ask me then."

"I'm asking you now." Mac lowered his voice. "It's her, isn't it? You've got some crazy idea that you can sweet-talk your way into Kate's bedroom."

"Shut up, MacMillan."

"You listen to me, cowboy. Kate Prescott belongs to this valley. We lost her once to a damned city slicker from California who threw away his life on a two-bit stunt. She doesn't need to get involved with some hotshot race car driver."

"Hit the patrol maintenance shop in Vegas on schedule next time, Mac. That way you won't have to worry about the cost of labor, here in Newton's Crossing or anywhere else."

Frank stepped aside and strode toward the café. He met Ev White coming out.

"Oh, Frank, I found the cutest little red car in Vegas. I've decided to take your advice and trade in my old car as soon as—"

"Ev, will you *move* it?" Mac shouted. "I haven't got all evening."

The teacher hurried to the cruiser, Mac following. "You remember what I said about driving," he called back.

"I owned a racing team, MacMillan. I built cars. That's in the past."

"You'll go back. They always do. Unless I've got you figured right and you really *are* a chicken. You just make damn sure you don't take Kate with you when you climb back into that car and that life."

Bobby shot around the side of the café. "Frank's not chicken!" he shouted. He kicked dust toward the departing cruiser, then choked as it settled on his tear-streaked face.

Frank bent and took the boy's shoulders. "What is it, kid? What's wrong?"

Then Kate was there. "It's my fault. I forgot the deadline—"

"It's too late, Mom!"

"No." Kate strode toward the garage and the pickup. "I should have checked the papers. I just forgot, that's all."

"I bet you didn't," Bobby shouted. "I bet you planned all along to miss it."

"Hey, kid, go easy on your mother."

Bobby wrenched away. "She thinks I'm a baby. I'm going to be *ten* in the fall!"

"Bobby, I'm sorry." Kate bit her lip and fumbled in her purse for the keys.

"Let me drive," Frank said. "You're as worked up as the boy."

They drove till twilight turned to darkness, the only sound the hum of the engine, the rush of the cooling air and now and then Bobby's sniffles.

"Someday, you'll have kids of your own," Kate said into the quietness. "You'll know how hard it is to be a parent and have to make tough decisions."

"If Dad was alive, *he* wouldn't have had any trouble deciding."

"Oh, Bobby, that's because your father never thought about the risks. He was never afraid for himself. How could he be afraid for others? Maybe that's why I stopped worrying about him. It seemed so useless...."

Frank reached an arm across the back of the seat, his hand brushing Kate's shoulder. At his touch, she eased.

"Dad was *brave*," Bobby insisted.

"Perhaps. But Bobby, taking risks isn't—"

"Frank's brave, too. He drove race cars. Officer MacMillan called him 'chicken,' but it's not true."

Frank was quiet for a long moment, sifting his memories, reaching for words. How could he make the boy understand? Did he have any right to try?

"There are different kinds of bravery, kid. Race car drivers sometimes try to prove they've got nerve by taking chances. Real courage has less to do with risk for the sake of itself, and more to do with giving up something for the sake of something else, or someone more important."

"Like you, Frank? Like staying at the crossing with me and Mom and giving up owning a racing team?"

Frank glanced at the boy, then trained his eyes back on the highway. "That was an easy choice," he said. "I'm not sure I'd call it bravery."

Bobby leaned back against the seat and sighed. "I guess I won't get a chance to prove I've got nerve *or* courage."

"We're headed for Mr. Peterson's house," Kate said. "The papers say that today's the deadline, but they don't say a thing about time. Besides, school's been closed for two days."

"What if he isn't even home? What if he's still at that meeting?"

"We'll find your principal if we have to comb the county," Frank said.

"You mean it?"

"You bet."

"Mom?"

"If this is what you want, Bobby, I'll support you all I can."

"I'll be careful, Mom." Bobby pulled a tissue from the box on the dash and blew his nose. "I'm sorry about what I said. And Mom? You don't have to come to the race with me. I know you don't like Rock Top Mountain."

Kate smiled wryly. Frank's eyes met hers, over Bobby's head, his brief glance reassuring.

They turned down the rough dirt road that dead-ended at the small adobe school on one side, the principal's ranch house on the other. Bobby jumped out of the truck as soon as it stopped.

Sam Peterson was home with his wife watching TV. He accepted the signed papers with no comment and wished Bobby luck. "How are you coming with your car, young man?"

"Just fine, sir. She's going to be a real beauty."

"I hear you're getting some special coaching." Peterson nodded toward Frank. "Do you think you can talk Mr. Vincenti here into helping us out on race day along with Bo and the other men?"

Bobby seemed to grow an inch taller. "Yes, sir! Frank, I know you're awful busy..."

Frank looked down into the face upturned to his. Earnest green eyes, a sunburned nose, a scattering of freckles...but he saw another face, heard another young voice from a long time ago. *Let me drive, Frank. I can do it.* A wave of trepidation swept over him then. He'd failed so miserably with Jesse. Was this another test? Maybe the biggest test of his life?

"I'll be there, kid. I'll make the time." The simple vow was one he'd keep, Frank knew. But why did he feel, down deep, that doing it would demand every ounce of courage he possessed?

"Give me a call," the principal said.

Kate was quiet as they headed back to the truck. "I'll drive," she said. "I'm okay now."

Bobby settled in between them, wiggling till his small shoulder was as close to Frank's arm as he could get it. Frank shifted to let him move closer.

She ought to be jealous, Kate thought, at seeing them touch with such easy affection, but her heart filled with warmth instead. It settled into that lonely place left since Bobby had grown too old for little-boy kisses.

Kate swung the truck around the circular driveway and headed back to the highway. "I've got just two questions for you, young man. First, what's this Ev White tells me about a spring project that's due? And second, was Frank in on the car from the beginning?"

Bobby squirmed. "He sure didn't want to be, huh, Frank? At first he didn't even want to look at my drawing. I think maybe Frank feels a little about cars the way you feel about Rock Top Mountain, Mom, maybe 'cause of his brother."

Bobby looked up and Frank stirred and looked down at the boy. "Hey, kid, you told me you'd mentioned the car to your mother."

"Yeah, and you said a mention wasn't enough. I should have listened. But now everything's out in the open. And Mom, Bo's great, but Frank's got special ideas. Bo says he must have been born with a wrench in his hand."

Frank chuckled and Kate laughed outright and reached to rough up Bobby's hair.

"Aw, Mom, you've got to stop doing that stuff. You never used to do stuff like that even to Dad."

"No," she said, remembering. They'd touched so little, she and Charlie, especially those last few months. Kate watched the highway but felt Frank's eyes.

"Let me tell you something, young man. Maybe you're all grown-up and maybe I'm going to have to get used to it, but I need a hug from my son now and then. That's how moms are."

As soon as they pulled into the Saguaro's parking lot, Bobby's small, thin arms slipped around her neck and a kiss light as a butterfly's grazed her cheek. For one precious moment, Kate hung on. Then Bobby pulled away and headed up toward the house.

Mattie came out of the café, wiping her hands on a towel. "Lucky you don't have school tomorrow," she called after Bobby. "There's a great late movie on TV tonight."

Kate touched Mattie's hand. "You're sure you don't mind?"

"Of course not. Bo's going to close the café then come up, too." Mattie squeezed Kate's hand and let it go, then smoothed her apron and fussed with the tie. "Bo felt real guilty about leaving us alone in the café all day, but he's been thinking . . . he'd like to help out in the garage full-time."

"But he doesn't want to ask?"

"More like he thinks the new cook you hired doesn't know sirloin from stew meat."

Kate laughed. "Two years ago he made his share of mistakes. If he wants to work in the garage we'll manage without him. Besides, the new cook has three kids, and he's been out of work six months. Jimmy can use the hours."

Mattie glanced at Frank, then down the dark highway. "All that talk about going back to bikes. Bo didn't mean to push, Frank. If you don't want him around—"

"It's not Bo's fault. The publicity about Indiana, the Long Beach race, the car...I've let it get to me, that's all."

"Things will be back to normal before we know it," Kate said.

"I'll certainly be glad of that." Mattie turned on her heel and headed back into the café.

The new cook was crimping crusts, and Bo was talking to a customer lingering at the back table. Something about the man was familiar, Kate thought, a ruddy face, neatly trimmed blond hair, easy smile. The man stood when Frank walked in. "Mr. Vincenti—"

"I'm off the clock, but Bo can help you. He'll be working the garage full-time from now on."

"You mean it, Frank? You sure you want the extra help?"

"Do *you* want to work like hell?"

Bo swept the café with a meaty hand. "This here is work. That over there is pure unadulterated play."

"Damn good attitude. See you tomorrow at dawn."

Kate was quiet as they walked hand in hand across the empty parking lot toward the old blue truck. Except for the sound of a semi far down the highway and the occasional crackle of the neon cactus sign, the evening was especially still. Even the wrens that usually chirped up a storm in the paloverde tree were silent.

Frank pressed Kate's hand and let it go. "I'll pump the gas."

She reached for the squeegee to scrub the truck's windshield. The water was clean and the wand was a bright blue plastic, new, like the stack of shiny gold oil cans and the big red-and-white sign in the garage window that advertised hours. She'd never seen that window look so clean. Beyond, in the dim yellow glow of the security light, she could see that the desk was orderly.

So much had changed in a few short weeks, though all for the better. The crossing was *alive* again.

Bo shouldered a tray of pies and headed for the oven in the dish room.

"Maybe I ought to go after him," the man at the table said. "He thought I was just another customer looking for help from the garage."

"You'd best not be botherin' Frank tonight," Bo said. "He's been working like hell. He deserves a break."

Mattie pulled off her apron and slung it over her shoulder. "You'd better not bother him at all, especially not with the kind of questions you're going to ask. You people don't seem to understand. He's trying to get away from that life—"

The man interrupted with a hearty laugh. "And *you* people don't seem to understand, either. This man has designed a race car that is going to move the whole world of auto design ahead by five years. I intend to get his story."

"We're closin' up, now, mister."

"You have rooms out back."

Mattie threw Bo a dark glance. "Sold out," the big cook said.

"Oh, come on, now. The place is empty except for all those cars parked over at the garage. You wouldn't be trying to discriminate—"

"All right," Mattie snapped. "Twenty-nine dollars a night. And we don't take credit cards."

"Thanks, I appreciate it. And look, I hope this doesn't get the two of you in trouble." The man tossed a fifty onto the counter. "Please, keep the change."

Grudgingly Mattie shoved a registration card his way and folded the bill into the register. She slammed the drawer just as the front screen door of the café flew open.

"Hey!" Bobby said. "I know who you are. I've seen you on TV."

The man stuck out his hand. "Andy Grant from Channel Twelve sports news. Good to meet you, son."

"Bobby, what do you—"

"We're out of popcorn, Mattie, and the movie's about to start."

"Bo and I will be along. We're just closing up."

"Going to watch a video tonight?"

"TV movie. It's a real good western."

"I've got something better out in the van. Something you might really enjoy. You into auto racing, son?"

* * *

The smell of lemon blossoms was heavy in the air, the sky above the bed of the truck thick with stars. Frank's deep breaths brushed Kate's bare shoulder with a gentleness hard to imagine, given the way he'd taken her, rough and hard, only an hour before. Kate drew a finger down the edge of his jaw. Frank's eyes eased open.

"Hate to wake you," she whispered.

He pulled her down to stroke her mouth with a languorous kiss. "Lady, you can wake me anytime."

Kate laughed, then suddenly serious, she said, "Cover me, Frank."

He reached for the blanket.

"No. Cover me with your body. Lie over me."

"Shy? I never would have guessed."

"Don't tease me. Just humor me now."

He swung his body carefully over hers, cradling her hips with his thighs, his stomach on hers, the dark, coarse hair of his chest brushing her breasts. He balanced his weight on his forearms. "That better?" he asked her.

"Much," she said. Kate closed her eyes and imagined that every pore in her skin was drawing him in. "I'm glad you didn't leave that Monday morning, after the fight with the bikers. I'd have tried to understand, but I'm glad you stayed."

"For this?" he asked her, drawing another long kiss from her lips.

"That's only part of it."

"And the rest?"

"Don't ask me now. I don't have words."

She eased out from under him and sat up, hugging her knees, looking up at the stars. Frank stroked the long slender bend of her spine, the swell at her hips.

For a long time, neither of them spoke. Then Kate reached for her clothes.

He caught her hand. "Not yet," he murmured. He pulled her down. "First this."

She felt him slide, swift and strong, inside her. He stilled a moment, leading her to expect the powerful, hard, quick thrusts. But instead, he held her hips, guiding them forward, then back, then forward again. She began to rock with him in a timeless rhythm as old as Eden. Kate closed her eyes. *Yes. First this.*

Then no more thinking. Just the quick, light movement of her body over his, the anchor of his hands at her hips, then a pause as he swept her over and down, still holding himself inside her.

Then she was the one arching up to meet his thrusts. Firm and fast he bore into her, accepting every movement she gave in return.

Then, just as she expected it to end, he moved more slowly, then slower still, till his thrusts brought long, low waves of exquisite pleasure.

"Ask me, Kate," he whispered. "Tell me what you want. You're always there for others, for me. Let me be here, now, for you."

She moaned in response and answered him the only way she knew how, with the rhythm of her hips as she rode the waves to ecstasy.

"Open your eyes, now," he said to her then.

It was all she could manage. Then she saw what he never could have told her with words—the sweet, still agony of release as it flushed his face, swept across his brow and plunged down the hard, pulsing chords of his arched neck. He climaxed within her. Kate reveled.

Nothing he could do, nothing he could say could change the way she felt. She was his. Completely, irrevocably, his.

That realization was enough to keep Kate silent all the way home.

"You okay?" he asked her when they pulled into the crossing.

She nodded, not looking up. "I was wrong about something," she said. "Remember the day I accused you of running? You could have said the same about me. I've done my share."

"You're not running from me."

"No."

"Sometimes it scares the hell out of me."

She looked up quickly. "Why?"

"Maybe someday you'll let me do something we'd both regret. I warned you once—"

"That the men in your family could not be trusted with *fragile* women?" Her light laughter stopped his answer. "Apparently you've started a new tradition."

He turned off the key and set the brake. "Not just with women, Kate."

At the pain in his voice, she touched his hand where it rested on the wheel.

He loosened his grip, turned his hand and took hers. "Bobby looks up to me. He's got some exaggerated idea—"

"Not so exaggerated."

"Believe me, it is. He's going to find out that I'm just a man, a very ordinary man."

"And then?"

"And then . . . you lose your ability to come between a boy and the things that can hurt him."

"You're talking about Jesse."

"Yes."

He looked away, out across the desert, and she knew that he was trying hard to hold back the tears that he thought would make him seem less of a man.

"It's all right, Frank," she whispered. "It's going to be all right."

He gathered her into his arms, and moments later his body shook with silent sobs.

An hour passed. He'd sat, just holding her hand, now and then bringing it to his lips to press a kiss on her fingers. By the end of it Kate knew that she didn't want to leave him, not now, not ever. If it weren't for Bobby, she'd have followed Frank to his room. She wanted to hold him through the night, to go on holding him forever.

Finally they got out of the truck and crossed the street, stopping in the circle of emerald light cast by the Saguaro sign. They shared just one kiss, long, lingering, but Kate knew that the memory of it would last a lifetime.

Then suddenly a door slammed, hard. The screen door to the house on the hill. A dark figure backed out onto the porch, a man. Mattie's stout silhouette followed. She was shouting something in an angry voice.

"Who in hell is that?" Frank said.

"I don't know, but I don't like—"

Frank took the railroad-tie steps by twos, Kate following close on his heels. The man stepped off the bottom step of the porch just as they reached it.

"Mr. Vincenti, I'm Andy Grant from Channel Twelve sports news in Vegas. I'd have introduced myself earlier, but—"

"It's a little late to be out doing interviews."

"Sure, well, I just got the assignment, and I don't like to let things get cold. I wonder if—"

"Frank! Guess what?" Bobby bounded out the door and swung down the steps. "Frank, Mr. Grant brought the neatest video tape. It shows your car, Frank, the one you built. The Silver Falcon? I got to see the whole race. Man, it was *so* exciting. Me and Bo—"

"That's enough, Bobby," Frank said. He turned to the man. "It seems to me that you've inserted yourself in a very personal way here."

"Hey, I'm just doing my job. That car of yours is a huge leap forward, Vincenti. You're hot news."

"I've sold the car. The new owners can give you all the details."

"But that's just it. They're not talking."

"That's not my problem."

"No, but it could be to your benefit. We're willing to make you a substantial offer—"

"Grant, you don't seem to understand. I've sold the car and the entire operation. I want nothing more to do with it. If the new owners want to keep the innovations under wraps till the car's won a few more races, that's understandable. They paid a handsome price for the right to do it."

"How much?" The man had whipped out a small pad and was already writing.

Bo lumbered out onto the porch and Mattie glared at him. "I told you we never should have let him come up to the house and show the tape."

Frank shot Bo an angry look and the big man shifted. "Uh, great race, Frank . . . uh, I'm sorry."

"It's not your fault."

"It was a *terrific* race, Frank. You should have seen it, Mom. I thought the red car was on fire, but Bo said, no, it's only steam. They run on methanol, Mom. It's not like gasoline. The flames are invisible. The driver wouldn't even know he'd caught fire, except he'd feel it through his racing suit. Isn't that right, Frank?"

"Bobby, I *said,* that's enough!" At Frank's stern tone, the boy hung his head.

Frank's face was ashen in the glow of the porch light. Kate let out the breath she'd been holding and reached for his hand, but Frank pulled away.

"They're used to danger, son," Andy Grant said. "For them it's just like going to work. It's just a job a lot like any other. Nine to five. Sometimes they come home late—"

"And sometimes they don't come home *at all.* My brother died doing that 'job.' Racing *is* dangerous. I want Bobby to understand—"

"But he enjoyed the tape, didn't you, son?"

Frank took a step forward, his hands clenched into fists. "Don't call the boy *son.*"

Kate stepped between them. "Frank?"

He looked into her eyes, seeing fear and a question. *Are you going to fight again?*

Was he going to settle another meaningless score the old Vincenti way? Provide Bobby with another shining example of how to be a man? Frank's gaze slid from Kate to the newsman. He *wanted* to do it. It would be a hell of a lot easier than trying to find words for feelings he could hardly name.

Tears glistened in Kate's eyes, and the urge to fight left Frank as suddenly as it had begun. He touched her cheek and stepped back, raised his hands in mock surrender, shrugged and turned away. He stepped off the porch and strode down the hill.

Andy Grant made a move to follow, but Bo pulled him back. "I wouldn't if I were you."

"What's gotten into the guy? He still having a hard time about his brother? You know, we were all pretty surprised to hear he'd sold the operation. Must have had something to do with that old story—what his father supposedly said about Frank being the brains, Jesse having the guts—"

"*Frank's* got guts," Bobby insisted.

"Sure, son, I didn't mean—"

"Just 'cause he's smart—"

Bo stepped forward. "Mr. Grant, I'm kickin' myself for invitin' you up here tonight with your videotape and your questions. We're just not interested. You get the message?"

"Okay, okay. I'll turn in. Maybe tomorrow... Mrs. Prescott, no one seems able to understand how Frank Vincenti ended up here in southeast Nevada, but I have a feeling you could answer that quite succinctly. I hope you'll talk to me tomorrow."

"An interview?" Kate laughed. "There's nothing to talk about. Newton's Crossing is a quiet place. That's what Frank needs right now."

"And I've come barging in and destroyed all that. Forgive me. Maybe tomorrow you'll give me a minute?"

"I don't think so. I run a café. It's been very busy lately."

"Yes, well..."

"Good night, Mr. Grant," Mattie said sternly.

They watched the man head down the hill, unlock his motel room door and disappear inside.

Mattie and Bo said an awkward good-night and left. Bobby lingered on the porch, hanging over the railing. They stood in silence looking down the hill toward the crossroads.

Heat hung like a shimmering sheet of black tinfoil over the café and the garage beyond. The red gas pumps bled their color into the night. Behind them, the yellow light in the office window flickered in the heat like a candle.

"I didn't mean to make him mad," Bobby said. His voice sounded small and lonely and Kate wanted to hug him but she knew he'd protest. Down in the garage, they heard the muted sound of the hydraulic lift.

"Frank sure works hard," Bobby said.

"Working on cars helps him. I think he's learned that it's one part of his old life he can keep."

"I don't understand, Mom. Frank loves cars but he doesn't want to talk about the best one he ever built."

"Sometimes talking makes the past too real."

"But it *is* real, Mom. Not talking about it won't make it go away."

She was thinking how wise Bobby's words really were, when suddenly the night sky lit with a silver streak. A jet screamed into the stillness. Kate froze, as she had all those years ago, and watched blinking wing strobe lights crest the top of the moonlit mountain.

Crazy, stupid fools. Pilots out to prove they were fearless, as though that would make them men. She'd call Lancaster in the morning and report them, if only for the sake of the families. An early reprimand might save some young pilot's life, and spare his wife the agony she'd endured, Kate thought.

"How come they do it, Mom?"

"I don't know, Bobby. I guess they don't think about tomorrow."

"I miss Dad sometimes. He used to laugh a whole lot, when he was around. I don't understand... there's so much I don't understand, Mom."

She crouched to Bobby's eye level. "Know what? There's a lot that I don't understand, either. But that's okay. We've got each other, the crossing, all these stars."

"And we've got Frank, too, don't we, Mom?"

His green eyes hovered between certainty and hopefulness, mirroring the feeling that fluttered in her heart. She wanted to say something comforting, something reassuring, but it would be wrong to lie, to herself, to her son.

Kate held Bobby's eyes with a steady gaze. "I don't know if he'll stay. I think he wants to. But we have to give him lots of room. He's been hurt, Bobby, on the inside where it doesn't show, because of what happened to his brother."

"The crossing's a good place to get well, Mom. Bo told me that just yesterday. He said it's the best place he's ever been for keeping healthy."

She hugged her son quickly, then let him go. "The crossing is good for lots of things, Bobby."

"And we're . . . not ever going to leave. Are we, Mom?" Bobby's voice had thickened, and Kate knew that there was more, some fear that he couldn't, or wouldn't, articulate.

She laughed to ease him. "We're not leaving unless something happens to the café and we have to, which means if I'm going to open on time I've got to get to bed. How about it?"

"Okay, Mom, but just one more thing. How come Frank told Mr. Grant not to call me 'son'?"

Kate was silent, thinking, feeling. A knowing too deep for words settled into her heart. "Why don't you find a time when Frank's not too busy and ask him that yourself, Bobby?"

"Maybe tomorrow—"

"*Not* tomorrow. You owe me an answer, young man. Remember? I asked you *two* questions in the car. Now, what's this about a spring project that's due?"

Bobby's thin shoulders slumped. "I've been working on it, honest, Mom. I'm going to do a display on spiders. I'm using those books you got me from the Summit City library."

"First thing tomorrow, before you get all involved with that derby car, I want you to get busy and finish."

"But, *Mom*—"

"No *buts* about it, young man."

Bobby groaned, opened the screen door and shuffled inside.

Kate had set her alarm for an hour earlier the following morning. She was showered, dressed and down the hill before the first light of dawn had warmed the horizon. She knocked on Andy Grant's door. "I'll give you an interview on two conditions," she said.

The man rubbed sleepy eyes. "Name them."

"First, don't mention the location of Newton's Crossing. We're not on the map, and—"

"You want to hang on to your peace and quiet. I can appreciate that. And the second condition?"

"Leave Frank alone. I'll make you breakfast, and we can talk. Then, later, after things have calmed down, I'll encourage Frank to call you."

"I don't know—"

"If I tell him your presence bothers me—"

"I know. He'll refuse to speak to me at all. All right. I'll do it your way, Mrs. Prescott. Just let me throw on my clothes."

"I'll go put on a pot of coffee."

Chapter Eleven

Andy Grant was gone before first light, but he reached Las Vegas in plenty of time to do the morning news. Though he kept his word and didn't mention the location of Newton's Crossing, the locals knew. They came out in droves.

By ten a crowd had gathered outside the garage, just to catch a glimpse of the man who'd sold off an Indy race car and gone to work fixing cars and trucks in the smallest town in southeast Nevada.

"I don't want the regular customers inconvenienced," Frank said to Bo. "See what you can do."

Bo's response was to lug a couple of old bench seats out under the front window, so some of the older men could sit down. Then somebody got the idea that cold drinks would be nice, and a couple of the high school girls headed for the café and came back with pitchers of iced tea.

Kids took turns pumping up their bike tires, and then they'd edge farther and farther into the garage till Bo shooed them out. He went over to the café at lunch, complaining.

"You'd think nobody worth gawkin' at ever came to the crossing."

"Well?" Mattie said.

"Heck, remember that time those movie stars came through?"

"'Came through' is right," Kate said. "As I remember they sent their limo driver in for coffee and donuts and then left in a cloud of dust."

Bo chuckled, wolfed down his burger and left with one for Frank. Kate, Jimmy and Mattie cooked and served without a break till half past two.

"You always said you wanted to see business pick up," Mattie grumbled as she unloaded another bin of dirty dishes. "Every planet in the universe must be in line."

"It'll pass," Kate said.

"Maybe. Meanwhile you'd better start emptying that cash drawer twice a day. Enough strange folks have been in and seen money sticking out the sides to invite a full-scale holdup. One of those bikers showed up last night."

"Which one? What did he want?"

"Nothing, no need to worry. The big guy was docile as a lamb, hardly spoke, just left you a letter. I stuck it under the coin tray in the register."

Kate dug out the envelope and tore it open on her way to the dish room to dial the house and check on

Bobby. She hadn't seen him since breakfast. Maybe for once he was following her directions precisely, though she hadn't meant that he should work so hard on the project he'd have to skip lunch at the café.

The phone rang at the house, and while she waited for Bobby to answer, Kate shook open the envelope. Five hundred-dollar bills fell out along with a note: *i'm real sorry. i dezerved what i got.*

She'd show the note to Frank, Kate thought. At least the fight he'd been so ashamed of had resulted in something positive.

The phone kept on ringing up at the house. Uneasy, Kate shifted the receiver to her other ear just as an errant breeze caught the dish room curtain and blew it inward. Kate glanced out the window at the units, Lady's water dish and the siphon, the old dog sleeping on the cool cement stoop underneath Frank's motel room window. *Where was Bobby?* Lady never left his side when he was at home.

Kate hung up the phone and headed out to the café just as Mac came in.

"Afternoon, Kate."

"Mac, did you see Bobby when you pulled up?" She brushed by him without waiting for an answer, heading toward the big center window.

A knot of men hung around the open bays. Others lounged on seats in the shade. Bobby would be among them or back there pestering Frank or off with the kids—

"I saw him this morning. Did he 'fess up?"

Kate turned from the window. "Confess? To what?"

Mac pulled at his ear. "I hate to rat on the boy, but I told him if he didn't tell you himself, I'd have to do it for him."

"Mac, *what* did Bobby do?"

"I caught him hitchhiking."

Her throat turned dry. She could hardly mumble, "When did you see him last?"

"Right after breakfast. I brought Ev in to pick up her car and stuck around for a second cup of coffee, otherwise I might have missed him. I was on my way out of town in the cruiser when I saw him try to flag down a semi just west of the stoplight. The trucker had sense enough to pass him by. I thought about writing up a ticket just to scare him."

"It's nearly two. He could be halfway to heaven-only-knows-where by now." Kate pushed open the café's door and ran across the street.

Frank was writing up an order in the office. Two long strides and she was in his arms.

"Bobby's gone. I've called the house. Mac said he saw him hitchhiking. Oh, Frank, what if—"

"Kate, calm down. Have you checked the house? Maybe he's up in the loft and can't hear the phone."

She pulled away to look out the window. "He didn't come down for lunch. Have you seen him, Frank?"

She turned back to see Frank just standing there. When he finally spoke his voice trembled. "He was here...this morning...early. He wanted to hang around. I...was sharp."

Bo had came in from the bays, wiping his hands. "The air this mornin' was thick as diesel smoke with chatter about the Silver Falcon. I thought Frank was goin' to blow a gasket. 'Bad influence on the kid,' he said.''

"*That's* an understatement if ever I heard one,'' Mac said, stepping in from the doorway. "You're a bad influence, all right, Vincenti. First thing the boy said when I stopped him this morning was, 'It's okay to hitchhike, that's how Frank got to the crossing.'''

Kate watched Frank's face drain of color. His silver blue eyes turned the color of lead.

Bo tossed the rag onto the desk. "Bobby never said a thing about hitchin' anywhere. Said he had some school project to finish.''

"That's it,'' Kate said. "He must have gone to the Summit City library for more books. I told him he had to get his report done first thing. It was crazy at the café this morning. He'd have known that I'd never be able to get off to take him.''

"Still, it ain't like the boy to go off without askin','' Bo said. "I'll head up to the house to check.''

"Look on the desk in the loft,'' Kate called after him. "See if his blue book bag is still there.''

"I'll get on the cruiser's radio, Kate. Maybe somebody's had word.''

Kate shivered and hugged herself. She didn't want to think what the word would be, if Mac found out that someone *did* know something.

The office door closed and Kate turned back to Frank. Agony etched his face with tired, dark lines. "Oh, *Frank,* Mac had *no* right to blame you like that. If Bobby's hitchhiking, it's not your fault.''

But Bobby would jump off a roof if he saw Frank do it. The thought hung in the air between them. Kate lowered her eyes.

Frank picked up the pencil, then tossed it across the desk. "Kids! You turn around and they're gone. Off doing something you've told them a thousand times to avoid."

Panic brushed Kate's heart like the phantom sweep of a bird's wing on a starless night. "Nothing is going to happen," she said carefully. "Bobby is going to be all right."

He glanced up at her. "I didn't mean—"

"Mrs. Prescott?" The office door had opened. One of the teenage girls leaned in. "Ma'am, someone said you were looking for your son."

"Have you seen Bobby?"

"I came in around ten with my boyfriend. We've been waiting to get an oil change. We're all off school for those meetings, you know, and—"

"Did you see Bobby?"

"Yes, ma'am. I saw him get into a car with a sort of thin-faced lady with reddish brown hair. It was a blue car, old, maybe—"

"Ev's car. Why would Bobby go off with Ev without telling me? And why would Ev—"

"No word, Kate." Mac came into the office, took off his hat and wiped his brow.

"Mac, Ev's taken Bobby."

"Are you sure? Hell, I never thought she'd—" The trooper fumbled with his hat, avoiding her eyes.

"What is it, Mac?"

"She...wasn't herself over breakfast, too quiet, mad about...oh, well. Then Bobby came in, talking about some guy that he'd invited up to the house last night while you were out."

"Andy Grant, that sportscaster?"

"I guess. Anyway, she lit into the kid. Went on for fifteen minutes about talking to strangers and how *somebody* had to make Bobby see the importance of school, maybe Child Services."

Kate felt the color drain from her face. "Ev wouldn't go that far."

MacMillan looked down at his shoes.

"I *know* she'd never call in the child welfare people, Mac."

Bo squeezed past MacMillan, into the office. "I checked the house. His book bag's gone."

"She's taken him to the Summit City library. I'm sure of it."

"I had dispatch call them. They haven't seen anyone fitting Bobby's description, and there's nothing charged out today on his card."

Kate slumped into the old swivel chair. "It's my fault. The café's been so busy. I've put work first. Ev's done this to teach me a lesson."

The trooper cleared his throat. "Evy's high-strung. It's been, well, worse than usual lately."

Kate leaned forward. "There's *something* you're not telling me, Mac."

"Aw, Kate, I don't want—"

"Tell me, *now*."

"It's just that Ev's got this idea. She mentioned it again last night. About how Bobby could have been hers, maybe should have been hers. How she'd been the one supposed to go out with Charlie, how she'd been with him the night before at her cousin's house. Kate, I never thought—''

Kate pushed back the chair so hard it nearly tipped over. "We've got to find them."

"It's a big state," Bo mumbled. "Where are we going to start lookin'?"

Frank reached for his dark glasses. "Her house would seem the logical place. Bo—"

"Go on. I can handle things here."

"We'll take the cruiser," Mac said. "We might need the light and the siren."

Kate pressed her lips together. Frank's eyes held the same uneasy question that she felt in the pit of her stomach. And something else. Something that reminded her of the day he'd come to the crossing.

Mac kept up a barrage of questions on the trip to Summit City. Twenty minutes later they were knocking at the front door of the small frame house in the suburbs. *Move to Summit City like I did. Put Bobby in a proper school.* It seemed just yesterday that she'd heard those words from Ev, Kate thought.

Mac knocked again but got no response. "She leaves a key under the step around back." He got red around his ears and started to explain.

"Let's just hurry," Kate said.

Mac unlocked the kitchen door, calling Ev's name. His voice echoed into the silence.

"I'll look around the yard and the garage," Mac said. "You two check through the house. There's a closet back in the bedroom where she keeps her luggage. You know the way?"

"It's been awhile since I've been here, but I'll find it." *Too long,* she thought. If she'd been a better friend . . .

Kate moved quickly through the sparse, clean rooms, Frank on her heels. On the old upright piano in the living room, she paused at the picture of Ev's mother.

"She was famous for that beehive hairstyle. She used to do all the ladies for miles around. Even my mother."

A sudden memory, so sharp she could smell her mother's perfume, hit Kate hard. Tears sprang to her eyes. "Mother never saw Bobby."

He reached out to hold her, but Kate shook her head. "We've got to hurry."

They found the small closet behind the bedroom door. Frank pulled the light chain and leaned in. "Night case, two matching suitcases and a garment bag."

Kate sighed with relief. "She can't be planning to go far or stay long."

He pulled the light chain and turned to face her. Kate didn't want to read the message in his eyes. *If she took Bobby, she wouldn't stop to pack.* She turned away, anxious to get out of the room.

On the way out, her eye caught the top of the bureau. Three pictures in polished silver frames stood grouped around a single plastic red rose in a crystal vase. One was of Ev from school days, laughing and waving; a smaller frame held Bobby's most recent school picture. A tall frame held a faded newspaper photograph. Charlie in his tux.

"It's my wedding picture from the *Summit City Sun,*" Kate said in surprise.

Frank picked up the frame. "She's carefully cut you out of the picture."

Her heart sank like a stone, but then Kate was suddenly calm. "I know this looks bad, but I also know Ev White. She would *not* kidnap my son." She took the frame from Frank and set it back on the bureau. "Charlie loved flirting with death. He'd have pulled Ev into his world and broken her heart. Or worse."

"Is there anything worse?"

His eyes held hers. Kate felt that she was watching a lifetime sift across his face. Then he turned away and shouldered out the door.

On the bedroom doorknob, she touched a man's tie, one she'd seen Mac wear. Poor Ev, spurned once by Charlie, now asking for it all over again.

It was all she could do to hold her tongue when they found Mac. Kate was glad when Frank spoke first. "What are the options? Where could she have taken him?"

"I can't believe she didn't take him to the library," Mac said. "Education's everything to Ev. She's always harping on the fact that Bobby isn't challenged enough. Yesterday morning when the training class ended, she tried to drag *me* out to the campus museum."

"In Vegas? Mac, I wonder if she's taken him there?"

"I'll make a call. Lock up the house, will you, Vincenti?"

A moment later Mac hung up the cruiser's mike. "Her car's in the lot. If I know Ev, the boy will get a good dose of Indian culture and be the better for it."

"If you know Ev, then you know she's not like the other women you've dated, Mac."

"Lord, you've got that right. I'm beginning to think she belongs in one of those looney—"

"If Ev's gone off the deep end, it's partly your fault. She's a dedicated teacher and that's left little room for anything else. Then you come along—"

"Now, wait just a minute—"

"You've led her on, Mac. Don't tell me differently. I saw your tie in her bedroom."

The trooper's face reddened and he pulled at his collar.

"Ev's a decent woman and she could make a man a good wife, unless you go spoiling her. She's had enough hurt. Don't make it worse."

Frank returned and climbed into the cruiser's back seat. "Hit those seat belts, people," Mac muttered.

An hour later they pulled into the museum's parking lot and spotted Ev's car immediately. Kate was out the door in a minute, Frank on her heels.

"I'll watch in case you miss them coming out," Mac said.

Frank held the doors and Kate rushed through them. Inside the cool building she stopped to allow her eyes to adjust to the softer light. The musty scent of old displays carried her back.

"Nothing's changed," she said. "I can almost feel Pop lifting me to his shoulders...." She swallowed hard. "What have I *ever* done comparable for Bobby? Horseback rides, the library, Saturday nights with popcorn and videos.'' She turned to Frank, but he seemed lost in his own thoughts, and judging from his face, they were even darker than hers.

Bobby trudged across the floor, Ev following. "Mom? Frank?'' Bobby's greeting was subdued.

Kate bent down but Bobby wouldn't meet her eyes. The look on his face told her that the last thing he needed was a lecture.

"He was trying to hitchhike to Summit City, Kate,'' Ev said. "I thought, well . . .''

"I was going to the library to get some more books for my report. I was going to surprise you, Mom. And I didn't want you to be mad at me, Frank.''

Frank crouched to the boy's eye level. For a long moment he said nothing. When he finally spoke his voice sounded empty, distant. "I wasn't . . . I'm not mad at you, kid.''

"I've been in your way.''

"No.'' He took Bobby's backpack off his shoulder and stood. "I'm the one who's been in the way,'' he said. "Along with my so-called entourage.''

That isn't true, Kate wanted to say, but words wouldn't come. She pulled her eyes from Frank's face and fastened them sternly on Bobby.

"If I've told you once, I've told you a million times, *never* hitchhike. You didn't deserve a trip to the museum on top of that.''

Bobby's eyes were wistful as he raised them to Frank. The tall man touched the boy's shoulder and nodded toward Kate.

"I'm sorry, Mom,'' Bobby said.

Kate's heart lurched and tears rose again. She pulled Bobby against her and hugged him hard to keep them from falling. "It's the crossing," she said. "We're just so darn far from anywhere."

Instead of drawing back, Bobby seemed to hug her harder for an instant. Then he broke away. "I've seen everything at the museum but the birds, Mom."

"They're the best part."

Kate rose, and Bobby shuffled across the room. Ev started to follow, then hesitated. "I...should have called."

Kate nodded. "I was worried sick, Ev."

"How did you find us?"

"Mac."

"Oh. He must have guessed where we'd gone. I told him last week that he'd love the baskets. He's fond of Indian arts and crafts, Kate. Such a macho guy, who'd ever believe it?"

"Mac's right outside. Why don't you go and invite him in?"

"Mac brought you to Vegas? You called the *police?* Kate, how *could* you? I'll never live this down! Kate, you spoil just *everything.*"

Ev rushed outside. Kate stood still, speechless.

She looked up at Frank. Everything about his face spelled exhaustion. And his eyes held a hurt that she could not bear. Had she somehow spoiled what they had, too?

"Look, Mom," Bobby called out. "I've never seen a falcon up close."

Kate and Frank crossed the room. "It's just like the one that Frank has tattooed on his shoulder," Bobby said. "Someday maybe I—"

"Tattoos are forever, kid," he said, his voice hard. "A choice you can't take back."

Bobby's lower lip quivered, but he drew himself up and squared his shoulders. "I'm going to make *good* choices from now on. Maybe I'll work on cars like you do, Frank. Maybe someday I'll even have a real race car—"

"Bobby, that's why Ev brought you here to the museum, I suspect. You've had nothing but cars on your mind since Trav brought that article to the crossing."

"I'm sorry, Mom. Please don't—"

"Look somewhere else for a model of what you want to do, and be, when you grow up, kid."

Bobby shot Frank a stricken look. Then he pushed by them, headed out the door.

Tears stung Kate's eyes. She stood still, fighting them back. If only she could fight back time, as well, stop it cold, or return it to that moment when it had seemed possible that the three of them . . . She looked up at Frank. In the new blue coveralls he looked like a man who'd chosen car racing for a living, a man who would miss the life, like Mac said, even if he never went back to it.

Frank touched her arm.

Kate pulled away. "I want my home and my son and my life back. I want things the way they were at the crossing before . . ." Tears choked off her words. Kate pushed out the door, into the late afternoon sunlight.

In the shade of a paloverde tree, Mac and Ev stood talking. Kate started toward them but Mac met her halfway. "I should talk to Ev," he said. "She took the boy without asking. If you were to file charges—"

"Don't be silly, Mac."

"She's feeling rocky. I don't think she ought to drive. Can you drive her car to the café? We'll meet you there."

"Of course," she managed to say.

She turned to look for her son, but Bobby was already climbing into the patrol car. Ev had one hand on his shoulder, helping him in.

She'd have her son back soon enough. But her life? The crossing? The years would fly by. He'd be off to college before she knew it. He'd leave sooner if she gave any thought to the boarding school Ev was pushing.

"Everything's changed. I don't know why I've stayed on," Kate said. "Sometimes it makes no sense at all."

"Maybe it makes all the sense in the world," Frank said. "It's not the crossing that has changed. And what I brought in can be taken back as soon as sunrise."

"No," she whispered. "I didn't mean—" But he'd taken the keys from her and headed for Ev's car.

"Kid okay?" he asked her as they got into the car.

"I think so."

They drove in silence for nearly half an hour. Frank watched the road, careful not to exceed the speed limit, careful when he passed, careful beyond a fault about his driving. It made Kate want to scream.

"You're angry that I gave Andy Grant the interview," she said.

Frank was silent.

"He isn't a bad fellow, just persistent, that's all."

Frank worked his jaw and gripped the steering wheel. Still he said nothing.

"He filled me in on a lot of things, Frank. The car is something special, not just another toy like I imagined. Apparently you have a gift—"

"I don't care about designing cars anymore."

"But that's ridiculous. You're throwing out the proverbial baby with the bathwater. Just because you've left racing—"

Frank laughed, the sound of it harsh and brittle. "I've left racing but it certainly hasn't left me, has it? Or the crossing. Or Bobby."

"You're blaming yourself. If anyone's to blame, it's me. Ev's partly right. I've put hanging on to the café first, always hoping for just the sort of turnaround that's taken place now that you've opened the garage. I never even thought about the impact on Bobby. I never see him these days. I don't keep my promises. If it hadn't been for you, he'd have missed those coyote pups that night we rode."

She glanced at him but his hard profile did not soften.

"Promises can get you into a hell of a lot of trouble. Maybe it's better not to make them, better not to get involved."

"With Bobby's derby race?"

"In general."

"You're talking about Jesse, too, aren't you? You think you let him down."

"My kid brother picked one hell of a time not to follow the rules. Even a nine-year-old boy like Bobby knows that a race car driver wears a fireproof suit."

"Andy Grant called your brother a hothead."

"My brother is *dead*."

"But it's not your fault, Frank. He died because he couldn't get the zipper on the fireproof suit to work. He could have taken time to get it moving."

"By then I'd have been at the track and kept him from ever going out."

"Maybe that time you'd have saved him, Frank, but eventually—"

"Kate, you don't understand what I'm saying. Jesse died because defying me was more important to him than his own life. We never worked it out, Kate. From the time he was a teenager and I let him get into that car—"

"But it was his *choice*. You've said that again and again, that it's all just a matter of choice."

"Jesse got into racing seriously because I walked away, and I walked away because my father accused me of being too cowardly to drive. It's about rebellion, Kate. It's as old as the hills and my family had it bad—physically, mentally, you name it."

"It doesn't have to be that way."

"No," he said, his voice softer. "When I see you with Bobby... when I saw you today... the way you talked *to* him, not *at* him, yet managed to be stern."

"Frank, your father must have tried to do the same for you. He was stubborn and his method wasn't the best. He used a lie. But maybe he thought if you found out just how good you really were... found it out too young..."

"I'd be hooked?"

"Something like that. Andy Grant said racing can be like cocaine. Some drivers feel a lack now and then, something vague that can't be named. They push it down with a dose of adrenaline out on the race-track."

"I'm not addicted. I never was."

"Exactly. And Bobby sees that. It confuses him, but he does see it. That counts for something. So did your father's lie, and your rebellion. Maybe your father said what he did to get you to rebel, and do it by leaving racing. Maybe that's what's made you so angry all these years. But maybe he *wanted* to get you out."

"And Jesse?"

"I suspect he knew that Jesse would never leave, was never meant to leave. Maybe racing *was* Jesse's thing, though not yours."

"Racing is *definitely* not Bobby's thing."

"In time he'll come to realize that. I've had trouble believing he would myself, but I know he will. It's just that right now, with all the excitement and public-ity—"

"It's going to end. I'm going to make sure of that." The tone of his voice was cold and hard. It made Kate's heart tremble.

"You're *not* going to rip into Andy Grant?"

His eyes were knives, cutting into hers. "You don't understand me at all, do you?"

The words cut her to the quick. That was the only thing she'd ever been good at—understanding. Now all she understood was her own limitations, the ones she'd met as a mother, as a wife.

They pulled into the crossing, to overflowing park-ing lots at both the café and the garage. He swung to the side of the road underneath the cactus sign, where Ev was waiting with Mac.

He cut the engine and turned to her. "I don't know what I'm going to do, Kate. I can't stand the effect I'm having on the crossing, on Bobby. I don't want to be responsible for—"

"Maybe you just don't want to be responsible, *period.*"

"Maybe." He set the emergency brake with a hard jerk. "I need to get away. If I go, things will calm down."

"How long?" she asked, her voice wooden.

He looked away. "I don't know." He tossed the keys out the window to Mac and got out of the car.

A harried Mattie appeared at the Saguaro's door with Jimmy. "Kate, we really need you in here."

"I'm coming," she said. It was all she could do to slide out of the car and head toward the café.

She stepped into chaos that nearly matched the turmoil she felt inside.

The café was packed. And the dish room sink was filled with dirty pots. Stacks of plates, cups and grimy bowls were heaped on the drain board. The ice bin stood open and empty. Inside the café, the jukebox blared, rattling every dish on the counter.

"I can help, Mom," Bobby said, rolling up his sleeves. Kate had an immediate vision of being hauled into court for violating child labor laws. Her own son would probably testify against her.

"Newton's Crossing used to be such a quiet place," Mattie muttered.

"Stick around till tomorrow. It will be again. Frank's taking a couple of days off."

"How come?" Bobby asked.

Kate didn't answer. She plugged the sink firmly and turned on the water for Bobby. "We need an automatic dishwasher."

"There's no room," Bobby answered.

"Well, maybe we need a bigger dish room, maybe a whole new café, maybe one *somewhere else*." She dumped in the soap and passed Bobby the first pot. At the sight of his small, pinched face, Kate wanted to cry.

It was dusk when Frank came in. She just turned around and he was there, staring at her with those same sharp, hard eyes that had met hers that first morning when he'd come into the café and into her life, laying both bare.

Applause and cheers broke out and a couple of the truckers even whistled. Bobby joined in from the back table where he'd been working on his report.

Kate stilled, his words in the air between them. *I have to get away for a while.* She turned away, then. In the dish room she stood at the back door, watching long shadows stretch across the parking lot toward the motel units, the house on the hill. She took deep breaths, trying to merge every cell in her body with the scene outside. The calm, expansive desert beyond seemed to beckon. So did the highway. Was she already letting go?

Kate filled the water pitcher and grabbed an empty tub, then headed back out to the café. Frank was gone, so was Bobby. She glanced out the big front window to see them crossing the street together, one tall man with a broad, strong back, one small boy, thin shoulders straight, hands thrust into his pockets.

Memories swept over her then. They gathered speed and rolled like a tumbleweed across her heart.

She saw all the times Bobby had turned to Frank, and all the times he'd responded. A touch, a quiet word, a helping hand. From now on, every time she looked out that big front window, she was going to see it all again.

Kate reached for the outdoor sign switch and threw it, and Frank and Bobby looked up as the tall two-armed cactus came to life. The small boy pointed at the sign, laughing about something, then turned toward the window and waved. Kate waved back. Frank stood still, chin tipped. Defiant till the end, she thought.

"Frank's not the man I knew two months ago. He's changed." Bo had come up behind her. "There's not so much loose anger bangin' around inside him no more."

"People don't change in two months," Kate said. "I'm not sure they really ever change at all."

"No, but maybe they sort of get free of themselves, you know?"

She glanced at Bo, then picked up the dish tub and began to clear the tables.

"It's this place," he said. Kate's hands stilled. "That garage, maybe. The way he talks to the customers. The way he handles the tools. The look on his face when he comes out from under a car. Even the way he heads back to the office now and then to tinker with one of his designs. Give him time, Kate. He'll make the right choice."

What *was* the right choice? For any of them? Someone at the counter called out for coffee. Kate turned away.

"Grandpop used to let me pass him the wrenches," Bobby said.

Frank eyed the small boy. "You got your project done, kid?"

"Oh, sure. Miss White told me I'd better do an extra page, but it went real quick. It's just like you said. If you think about *why* instead of just how things happen—"

"The café's busy. Your mom could use help."

"I got all those pots and dishes done up. I like to do dishes. It gives me time to think. And sometimes I look out the dish room window toward the motel units and I see the *weirdest* things."

"Such as?"

"Once I saw lightning strike right over the top of the roof of our house. I watched for the walls to explode and burn up. Course that didn't happen 'cause the lightning was far away. It took the thunder a real long time to get here. Do you think maybe we need a lightning rod on our roof, Frank? Do you think maybe you and I could fix one up?"

Frank rose and reached for a cloth to wipe the wrench and his hands. He tried to avoid looking into the earnest green eyes in the small face upturned to his. "Bobby," he said, "remember that time early on when I told you I couldn't make any promises?"

"Sure, Frank, but I'm not worried. If something comes up and you get too busy to help out at the derby race, I'll understand. My dad used to promise to pick me up from kindergarten all the time, then he'd get busy at work and Mom would have to come. I used to get so mad . . . course I was just a little kid then."

Bobby had been holding one of the new wrenches, shining it on the leg of his jeans, shoving it into his small back pocket then taking it out and holding it up to the light. Frank held out his hand for the wrench, and Bobby gave it to him. He squatted on his heels to take the boy's shoulders.

"Bobby, I don't think . . . I've got to go away for a few days, kid."

The boy's eyes got wide for a moment, then settled. "I know, Mom said. It's okay. When you get back—"

"There's a chance . . . I've got some thinking to do—"

"Are you going to go see your car in a race? Maybe help the team get ready for Indianapolis? Mr. Grant said—"

"I'm not going back to racing. Bobby, *listen* to what I am saying. *I might not come back.*"

The green eyes filled with tears and Bobby tore away to hide them. "It's Mom. She's making you go."

"No, Bobby."

"She doesn't like race cars and stuff that goes fast. How come she can't let other people like them? How come she can't let—"

"Your mother has *nothing* to do with my decision, son. *Neither* do you." It felt like the first real lie he'd ever told. But maybe, like his father's lie—

"*You* called me 'son.' You got mad at Mr. Grant when he did that." Bobby turned and pushed out through the garage door and sprinted across the road.

Let Jesse do the driving from now on, Frank heard his father say.

"Jesse's dead, Dad. There's only me."

He could almost see the bent shoulders, the lined, drawn face smudged with grease. Had Kate been right? What was a father, anyway? What did it mean to call a boy *son?*

Chapter Twelve

"One more day like this and we're going to have to hire another cook *and* another waitress," Mattie said, scrubbing hard on the grill. "If the crossing doesn't get back to normal soon—"

The back screen door in the dish room slammed, cutting off her words. "Mom?" Bobby called out.

"Newton's Crossing will never be *normal* again," Kate said. "I'm thinking about getting as far away from this place as that highway will carry me. Have you ever thought about giving up waitressing for *owning* a café, Mattie Thompson?"

"*Mom!*" Her son shouted the single word from the dish room doorway, then turned and ran.

Kate tore off her apron and headed for the door. And then she was running across the emptying parking lot, calling out Bobby's name.

The small boy headed for the house on the hill, Lady at his heels. Kate ran after him. He stumbled once, and Lady barked, then Bobby got up and ran again.

Kate caught up with him on the porch. His hands were scraped raw as her heart. She caught her son in her arms and held on. He struggled, tossing his small body from side to side. He cried till Lady came up to the stairs and stood at the bottom of them, howling. Finally exhausted, Bobby crumpled to a heap in her arms. Kate sank to the floor, holding her son.

She held him and rocked him, the way she hadn't done in years, rocking her own body, too.

"Is that why you're sending me away, Mom? 'Cause you want to leave the crossing? I'd *hate* that school, I know it, I don't care what Miss White says. But if you want me to go... Mom, just please don't sell the Saguaro Café. I can go anywhere and do anything I have to do, as long as I've got you and the crossing to come home to."

"Bobby, what on earth—"

"She told me about the boarding school on the way to the museum, Mom. I didn't want to believe her, but I'd seen that folder in your desk."

"The brochure of the Desert Sands Boarding School? But I—"

"It looks like an awful place, Mom. The folder said the grounds are all lit up at night for security. You'd never be able to see the stars, Mom, not with all that light."

"Bobby, listen to me. Never in a million years would I send you to a place like that. I'm not sending you anywhere. I'm your mother and you're stuck with me, like it or not."

He clung to her tightly. Then he whispered, "Are we leaving Newton's Crossing?"

Kate laughed through her tears. "Oh, Bobby, adults say stupid things sometimes. It's a kind of running away that we do in our heads when we know we can't do it for real."

Bobby wiped his sleeve across his face. "Like that time I chased the truck when I thought Frank was leaving? I didn't want him to go, but I couldn't say it right, so I said something dumb."

She nodded, unable to speak.

"I asked Frank to take me with him. I'm sorry, Mom. I didn't really mean it. I wouldn't have run away. I don't ever want to leave the crossing."

Kate hugged her son. "I'm sorry, too, Bobby. And you can stop worrying. For better or for worse, Newton's Crossing is going to be home forever. But some things have to change. You and I are going to spend more time together, even if I have to close the café early. And no more secrets. If you're worried about something, you've got to tell me right off. Don't let it go festering. Promise?"

Bobby nodded, quiet. "Mom, why does Frank have to leave? He says he might not be back. I don't understand...."

Kate was silent, thinking of the man who'd stood on the porch where she and Bobby sat now. *I hope to God I've changed, Kate.* She held Bobby close and brushed the top of his head with a kiss.

"I don't know, Bobby. I just don't know."

At the sound of footsteps on the path, Bobby wiped the last of his tears on his sleeve and peered out into the darkness. The tall silhouette was unmistakable. The boy scrambled to his feet. Kate rose, too.

"I ran away. I'm sorry," Bobby said.

Frank hooked one boot on the bottom step and looked up at the boy, his mother. "Running away is best sometimes."

"I know, like when you're outnumbered, or when you've got to go for help."

"Other times, too. Violence is rarely the answer, kid. You remember *that,* not what you saw that night outside the café."

Bobby nodded, subdued.

"Come inside?" Kate said softly.

"No. Thanks. This won't take long." He sat down on the porch at the top of the steps, one knee bent, his back to the house. Bobby hesitated, then sat down on the step below him. Slowly, tentatively, the boy lifted his hand in the high-five salute they were always sharing.

Frank matched his own hand to Bobby's, palm to palm.

The boy sighed. "Guess it's going to be an awfully long time before my hands grow as big as yours."

Frank leaned back, looking out at the crossing, then up at the stars. "Time goes fast, kid. One day you're playing with dogs and building derby cars, and the next day you're off to college. You come home and your hands are just as big as your father's . . . or your mother's."

Kate's eyes met his, soft, forgiving. God, how he was going to miss those eyes of hers. How would he ever—

"I'll be glad when I grow up. I'll be able to do lots of things."

"Anything *you* choose. That's what I came up here to tell you, Bobby. They're *your* hands. You think long and haid about how you want to put them to use.''

''Sometimes I think I'd like to study spiders when I grow up. Do you think a person could do that for their whole life?'' Bobby yawned and leaned his head against Frank's leg.

''Why not? The world could use another authority on something with sense enough to get around under its own locomotion.''

''How are you going to get where you're going, Frank? You haven't even got a motorbike like Bo.''

''I'll hitchhike, but I'll do it with one of the drivers I've met. Even adults should be careful.''

Bobby yawned again. ''Tomorrow?'' he said sleepily.

Frank's throat tightened. It was a long minute before he could speak, and then only in a whisper. ''I'll be gone before you get up, son.''

Son. He'd said it again. Without meaning to. Yet the single word seemed to settle in his heart, pushing out the last of his anger. His eyes burned, and he closed them.

Bobby hadn't answered. His head was heavy against Frank's leg. ''He's asleep,'' Kate said softly. ''I'll just—''

''Let me,'' Frank said. He rose, lifting the boy carefully. Kate held the screen door.

He carried Bobby to his bedroom, took off the boy's sneakers and jeans and then pulled the thin blanket up over his shoulders. Kate switched off the low lamp beside Bobby's bed.

Frank stood still, the soft darkness spreading over the boy, the room, himself and Kate. He turned and touched her cheek.

She took his hand. "Come out to the porch," she whispered.

They stood at the railing looking out. The crossing was quiet except for a few cars and a truck or two outside the café. The air around the porch was still.

Suddenly, above them, a bright star fell. Kate caught her breath. "Pop used to say, 'Be careful what you wish for, you're just likely to get it.'"

"Your father was wise."

"Maybe yours was, too."

"In his way."

"I wonder if Bobby really will grow up to study spiders?"

"He has lots of time to decide."

"What about us, Frank? I wish—" She broke off and laughed, the sound of it sad. "Remember that first night on the porch? I said that I'd learned to accept whatever comes. But that's not true. I'm an ordinary woman who looks up at a falling star and makes a silly, ordinary wish."

He turned, wanting to take her in his arms, wanting to hold her close, wanting to ask her what she'd wished for, to tell her that whatever it was it couldn't be silly, or ordinary. But he stood still.

"I've got to stop running, Kate."

"And staying here would be running?"

"I don't know. I've got to find out." He lingered a few minutes more, longer than he should have. "Good night," he said finally, then strode down the porch steps and into the darkness.

At the bottom of the hill, his hand on the door to his room, Frank turned and looked back, but the light on the porch at the house on the hill had already gone out.

Emptiness settled inside him. He knew it would last, maybe until he'd put a thousand miles between himself and Newton's Crossing, Nevada, maybe till he'd lived twice again as many days.

For now, he just wanted morning to come. He wanted to get into a passing semi and give himself over to destiny. But what sort of destiny would it be? And what would it be worth without Kate? Without the boy?

Frank let himself into his room, not bothering to turn on the light. He stripped off his shirt, threw back the spread and lay down on the bed. In the darkness he touched the falcon on his shoulder.

Tattoos are forever, Jesse.

So? A guy's got to have something that lasts, doesn't he? Isn't that what you're always telling me, Frank?

He could hear Jesse's cajoling laughter as though it were yesterday, feel the sultry summer night, smell the odor of magnolias mixed with the sharp scent of hot needles and skin.

Come on, Frank. It'll be like becoming blood brothers. Like in the Old West.

This is New Orleans, and we're already brothers.

You know what I mean.

He *had* known, or thought he had known, and he'd gone with Jesse into the small, smoky tattoo parlor, and they'd chosen the design, then taken turns watching each other grit teeth against the searing pain.

And for what? For a link that would finally give them something in common? A family tie that would last, even beyond the grave?

Nothing lasts, Frank thought. Jesse's falcon was ashes. In the world of racing, victory was only as enduring as your next defeat, and that was the only world that he had ever known. Everything ended, *everything.* Except, perhaps, if he wanted it badly enough, if he *chose*...

The parking lot was empty by the time Kate got back to the café. Mattie was at the register cashing out, and Bo had just finished mopping the floors.

"I got the pies left to do," the big man grumbled. "Busy as Jimmy and Mattie were, they never got time."

"It's late, Bo. We'll skip the baking tonight."

"We don't ever start the day with no dessert."

"You can't work from dawn till dusk fixing cars and then come here and bake pies," Kate said. "Go home, get some rest. Take Mattie with you. She's supposed to get off at three and that hasn't happened in days."

The big man stood still, chewing his lip. Finally he stomped out to the dish room. Kate heard the sound of water and the swish of the mop. But in a moment Bo was back.

"Jimmy's not up to snuff. I ought to come back and help out."

"He needs more time, that's all. And things will be quieter tomorrow."

"Frank's goin' away. Business at the garage will slack off."

"None too soon. You'll have your hands full with the orders already taken."

"I don't know...." Bo shrugged and stuffed his hands into his pockets. "It ain't the same when

Frank's not there . . . still, we could sure use the extra money."

Mattie slammed the register drawer. "I don't care two hoots about money."

"Oh, come on, Mattie. You've always got your nose in that catalog."

"Looking and liking isn't the same as wanting, Bo. And at least I'm not mooning after some extra part for a beat-up motorcycle."

The big man snorted and lumbered back out to the dish room. A moment later they heard the back screen door slam, hard.

"The old Bo is back, ornery as ever," Mattie said.

"And the old Mattie's back, too, it seems," Kate said gently.

Mattie ducked her head for a moment. Then she pulled off her apron and swept it into a ball. "Neither of us wants to see Frank go."

"I know. I don't want him to go, either."

"Did you tell him that?"

"In so many words."

"How about just two—*Don't leave.*"

Kate began to stack dishes on the shelf, one after another. "If you care about a man . . . if you love him or even think you do . . . after Charlie died the only thing I had left to feel good about, besides Bobby, was that I'd never stood in my husband's way."

"Don't guess that did much good since he went ahead and smeared himself all over that mountain."

"No," Kate said, "it never did any good at all."

An hour later Kate locked the back door of the café and stepped out into the darkness. A warm wind blew. There were no stars, no moon anymore. The air smelled thick with rain that would probably blow on through. Tomorrow they'd wake up to parched desert air and the first real heat of summer. Sand swirled at Kate's feet and stung her ankles.

She wanted to head up the hill, crawl into bed, begin to forget. Or...walk across the parking lot, knock on Frank's door and tell him... *tell* him...

But she'd wanted to sell the café and run to the ends of the earth, too. That feeling had passed. This one would pass, also, she told herself. She stepped into the parking lot, heading toward the path and the house on the hill.

A tumbleweed came out of nowhere and swept across her path. It rolled to the edge of the road then down toward the blinking red light at the crossing. Where would it stop? she wondered. Where would *he* stop? Or would Frank just keep on going? Just keep moving from town to town, city to city, searching for... what?

I don't know what the hell I want, she heard him say again. *Do you?*

The breeze had picked up hour by hour outside the motel room walls. Frank lay there listening to it. He might have missed the knock at his door, so soft, so gentle it could have been the wind.

"Frank?"

He was up in an instant, throwing open the door.

"Frank, I—"

He folded Kate in his arms. The smell of her hair made him ache inside, and the brush of her shirt and breasts against his bare chest made his throat burn with fire.

"Kate, *Kate,* I don't know why I have to do this. Please, please, tell me not to do it."

She wanted to say it. She thought of the first moment she'd seen him, when he'd come into the café, his face unreadable except for the hint of defiance in his eyes. Now those eyes held only pain. She wanted to tell him anything, so long as it would take away that look. *Stay,* she tried to say with her eyes.

"Oh, Frank, Bobby needs you . . . I need you so."

He covered her mouth with his, drinking in her words, tasting her need, mixing her breath with his own, then giving it back to her with deeper, hungrier kisses.

"I need you, too, Kate. I need you so very much."

She turned from him then, and slipped out of her shirt, her jeans.

"Kate, are you sure? How can either of us live with the memory?"

"How can I live without it? You're going away. I don't know if you'll ever come back." She stepped close to him, touching his hands, inviting his caress.

"I have no right—"

"It's not about that," she whispered. "Nor about my wanting to hold on to you. Please don't believe—"

He kissed her mouth to stop the words, then touched her breasts, her belly, the warmth below. He lifted her and carried her across the room to the bed.

She was restless in his arms. She moved over him, under him, paused to pleasure him with kisses. Caressing, touching, she hardly allowed him to reciprocate. The heat of her body matched her invitation, but something elusive was missing. It held her back.

She cried out again and again as he entered her and stroked.

But he knew she was not ready.

"It's nothing. I'm tired," she whispered. "Don't wait..."

"Kate, tell me what you want."

"Please, Frank, I want you to feel—"

"*Tell* me, Kate. Tell me what *you* want to feel. Tell me what I can do, what I can give you."

"Your touch, just your touch. Here, and here." She guided his hands to her breasts, to the hard stiff peaks of her nipples.

"That's good, Kate. Don't stop. Don't try to give. You *always* give. Let me do it now."

She lay back then, with a long, sweet sigh, and opened herself completely to his touch and his kiss and his endless caress.

And it was good for her, she told him, over and over, and better than it had ever been for him. Better than he had ever imagined that it could be.

Fatigue claimed him then. He slept soundly, as though there'd be no tomorrow.

And sometime in the night, Kate rose and returned to the house on the hill.

He thought he saw her drift away from him in his dream. He wanted to call out to her. He dreamed that he said the words. *I love you, Kate.*

Kate was up long before dawn. She knew Frank was gone. She'd awakened earlier to the sound of a slowing semi, the squeal of its brakes, the hard slam of a heavy door, then the slow acceleration up the mountain, and finally the faint farewell of a distant air horn.

When she came out of the shower, Kate found Bobby working at the kitchen table.

"You're up awfully early."

"I'm working on my vocabulary words. I want to get them all right on Friday's spelling test. I got all but one last week."

"Bobby, school is important, but—"

"I'm going to do real good this term, Mom. I'm going to work hard and bring up my grades. You're going to be proud of me."

"I'm proud of you already."

"Miss White says I'm not working up to my potential. But I can do it. And... well, I thought maybe if I got my work done early, then after school I'd finish up that last coat of paint on my derby car."

Kate smiled. "Now the truth comes out."

Bobby grinned sheepishly. "Frank says it's important to try to finish what you start. I'm not the greatest at that, Mom. I get all interested in putting together a model, but then something else comes along...well, you know what I mean."

"I guess I do," Kate said gently. "Don't work too long. Come down to the café in time for breakfast."

When had it happened? she wondered as she walked down the hill in the predawn darkness. When had this sturdy, small boy who'd asked question after question suddenly started answering them for himself? Or had it been happening little by little all along, while she'd kept busy with the café and the crossing? Frank was so right. Childhood lasts only a moment.

Frank.

The last thing she wanted to face was the empty garage, the row of motel rooms, the silent café. She paused on the path to look down across the street to the garage.

The old red gas pumps beckoned. *Here we are,* they seemed to say. *Right where you left us. Not everything changes.*

But there was no light in the window. Only the big green cactus sign still burned brightly into the last wisps of night. She would see Frank standing beneath it for the rest of her life, Kate thought.

And so she remembered with all the intensity that she could muster, that first night on the porch, then later the sight of his torso, naked to the waist, muscles flexing in his bedroom mirror as he bent over the sink with his jeans. She remembered the sudden, surprising warmth of his skin the night in the rain when his bare chest had come into contact with her breasts. She remembered the taste of his mouth in the starlit grove, hard and alive on hers, then softer, then hard again till she'd yielded and taken the pulsing beat of his body into hers.

She thought of the falcon on his shoulder, the silver bird that had covered them both just a few short hours ago, and she remembered the living, breathing man, as though in doing it with all her heart, mind, body and soul, she could ensure his return by sheer power of will.

She had let him go, but at least she would not kid herself into thinking that it didn't matter. That would be a lie, Kate knew, and she was not going to lie to herself or to anyone else about her feelings ever again.

She straightened her shoulders. The new cook was going to be off and Bo would be busy in the garage. They'd have their hands full, with or without the big cook. Kate quickened her pace.

She caught the smell of simmering bacon. When she pushed into the café, Bo was at the griddle, flipping sizzling strips. "Damn fool hungry people nearly cleaned us out," he said, cocking his head toward the dish room. "I found one crate of eggs, two measly pounds of bacon and about enough bread to last through to ten o'clock. But you know what, Kate? We got plenty of something called 'grits.' Two cases to be exact. Where the hell did we get that stuff?"

Bo turned, his big eyes soft. "He'll be back, Kate. Just wait and see."

She hugged Bo around his plump middle, then broke away. "Some trucker brought in the grits. Said he was homesick and wanted to make sure we could feed him his usual breakfast."

"If he was homesick he just ought to have stayed *home,*" Bo said. He glanced down the counter, caught Mattie's quiet smile and returned it with a shy one of his own.

"Let's get this breakfast show on the road," Mattie said. "You've got work to do across the street. A guy with bad brakes came in just as Frank was rolling out. We put the man up at the motel."

"Did Frank say where he was going?"

"He was real distant. Said he wasn't sure."

Maybe he'd go somewhere to someone who could let him be himself, Kate thought, to someone who could let him go when it was time.

She moved toward the window. A thin band of pink rimmed the horizon. She reached for the cactus sign light switch, then stopped. Maybe if she left the sign lit . . . *crazy,* she thought and switched the sign off.

How many days, weeks, even months would it take before she stopped watching and waiting?

The café began to fill. Mattie made a big sign for the front window, Hot Grits Special Today. A few customers actually ordered it, which set Bo grumbling about how he was too darn old to learn to cook new stuff.

Ev came in, minus the heavy makeup and extreme hairstyle, looking like herself again, Kate thought. Ev poured her own coffee, then insisted on carrying the empty pot back to the dish room.

"It's high time I started making myself useful around here," Ev said as she measured out fresh coffee. "Otherwise one of these days you're going to kick me out."

"The Saguaro wouldn't be the same without you, Ev."

Ev's smile was wistful and genuine. "Kate... I'm sorry. I should never have taken Bobby without asking you. I've been a little crazy lately, what with Mac... and there's something you ought to know. I... I've always felt that Charlie..."

"I know."

"Did Charlie *tell?*"

"He never said a word. But I should have guessed. Oh, Ev, all these years... Charlie ruined my life by leaving on a whim, and he ruined yours by coming in on another one."

"I let my own festering jealousy do that." Ev pulled a tissue out of her pocket and blew her nose.

"Come on," Kate said. "Let's get you breakfast."

"I'll have a bowl of those grits, Bo," Ev said as she passed the cook. "No rush, take your time."

"Uh, sure, ma'am."

When Bobby came in, Ev called him over. "You'll have to take the school bus from now on. I don't want the other children thinking that you're teacher's pet. I'm afraid the special favors are going to have to stop, Bobby."

"That's okay, Miss White. I *like*—I mean, I don't mind the bus. I'll get one of my friends to give me my spelling words."

The front screen door opened and a rancher came in, followed by MacMillan. Mac stood near the door, turning his hat in his hands.

"Sit down," Ev said. "We're having grits. They're very good for the digestion. Just because I told you my house was off-limits doesn't mean we can't be friends."

Mac eased himself into the chair opposite. "I was thinking, Evy. That front fence of yours needs painting."

"I can paint my own fences, thank you. Of course . . . help is always nice."

Kate poured Ev's coffee, then Mac's. Ev passed him the cream and two sugars.

Some things *were* going to work out, Kate thought. Sooner or later Miss Uptight White was going to have her way with the state of Nevada.

By ten she knew that the day would be hot. They were going to need the cooler. And at three o'clock when she flipped the switch to turn it on, Kate knew she wouldn't have to worry about the motor cutting out. Everything at the crossing was in good shape now. She even had the money to fix the front window, thanks to the contrite biker.

"If there's money left over after the window, let's get the neon sign fixed," Mattie said. "If business keeps up we just might need that No on the Vacancy sign now and then."

Back at the rear table, Bobby laughed. "That makes me think of what Frank said about the sign. '*Room* makes sense. That's one thing Nevada's got plenty of.' "

The laughter was light, then it quieted. Kate lingered at the window. Bobby bent over his schoolbooks. Bo reached for another order off the clips above the grill. The café's gentle conversation drifted in to comfort Kate, easing her heart.

Another night passed, then morning inched toward afternoon and then on to evening again. Kate kept returning to the window, watching the sky turn gold, then pink, then a deep magenta, a color she knew would last only moments. She stood there, taking it in. That was all she could do now, Kate thought. Live each day. Take whatever the crossing delivered. Let her heart heal.

She'd just turned on the cactus sign when she heard it. The low hum of an engine. The car was just a dot on the darkening horizon, winding down the road from Rock Top Mountain. But it was moving very fast.

Kate's heart set up a sudden hard rhythm, pulling her feelings with it. First wrenching, then hopeful. Useless, *worth everything*.

Half a mile out she saw that it wasn't a car at all, but a truck. At the crossroads the blinking red light bounced off the hood of a brand new Chevy pickup. Silver blue. Like his eyes.

A moment later Frank Vincenti walked through the door of the Saguaro Café.

Everyone quieted and turned, except for Bobby, intent on his homework. You could hear a cactus flower open, Kate thought. It was just that still.

He wore jeans, dusty boots and a faded denim jacket, dark glasses and a blue baseball cap, *Vincenti Racing* across the crown. His black leather backpack hung from one shoulder.

Frank stood still as stone. He looked at Kate, and she looked back.

"Frank!" Bobby almost knocked over his chair in his eagerness to reach the door. The tall man bent down and put the hat on Bobby's head.

"Wow! Can I keep it, Frank?"

"It's yours, kid."

"I knew you'd come back."

He grinned at the boy. "There's a race coming up, down the hill on the south side of Rock Top Mountain. You and I and Bo are going to make one darn fine team."

Bobby laughed and hugged Frank hard. Then Frank rose. He strode past Kate, over to the register. "Got a room, ma'am?" he asked Mattie. "I figure I'll be needing it indefinitely."

Kate was in his arms then. Laughter, tears and words all tumbled over one another. Where had he been? Where—

Tires squealed and gravel flew against the front window, and a minute later Mac strode into the café, Ev at his heels.

"I've got you now, Vincenti. You're going to pay up big. Don't try to tell me you weren't doing twenty plus the limit when you passed that turnoff."

A communal groan rose from the customers, and Mac turned his usual shade of crimson. "I got me a witness, right here."

"And what was Miss White doing in your cruiser?" Bo asked as he flipped hamburgers. "Bet you weren't payin' real close attention to that radar gun, *Officer* MacMillan."

Ev laughed out loud. "I'll testify to that," she said. "One must *always* tell the truth."

Frank smiled. "The lady has a point," he said. "The truth is, I love you, Kate Prescott."

Kate's eyes filled and spilled over, but she did not look away from his face. "I don't want to hold you back. I couldn't bear it if—"

He laughed, then, and pulled her to himself. "Kate, it's taken me a lifetime to learn it. Don't you know it yet? We're shaped by the people we love. There's nothing wrong with that, not as long as what's at the center of the wheel is honest and strong."

He swept her up in his arms and carried her out the front door. Everyone in the café followed, Bo and Mattie, Bobby, Ev and Mac, the scattering of customers.

"I've got some ideas," Frank said. "Desert light is strong, consistent and clear, great on a drafting table. I could build a small design operation, hook up by computer to the big boys in Detroit. When I get bored with that I'll go out and get my hands dirty with Bo in the garage. Do you think Newton's Crossing could use the business, Kate? I might need to hire—"

She kissed him, hard, closing off his words.

A cheer went up then, from everyone watching. It echoed down the highway.

"You were so right, Kate," Frank whispered. "I scattered Jesse's ashes. *Pacific* does means *peaceful*, but only if you take it with you."

"I love you, Frank."

"Then, will you marry me? I'll love you forever, Kate. And I'll do my best with Bobby."

She hugged him hard, and he whirled her around and around and around, till the horizon became a single, endless, moving ribbon, tying her family together.

* * * * *

FORTUNE'S Children™

Bestselling Author
LISA
JACKSON

Continues the twelve-book series—FORTUNE'S CHILDREN
in August 1996 with Book Two

THE MILLIONAIRE AND THE COWGIRL

When playboy millionaire Kyle Fortune inherited a Wyoming
ranch from his grandmother, he never expected to come
face-to-face with Samantha Rawlings, the willful woman
he'd never forgotten...and the daughter he'd never known.
Although Kyle enjoyed his jet-setting life-style, Samantha and
Caitlyn made him yearn for hearth and home.

MEET THE FORTUNES—a family whose legacy is greater than
riches. Because where there's a will...there's a *wedding!*

A CASTING CALL TO
ALL FORTUNE'S CHILDREN FANS!
If you are truly one of the fortunate
few, you may win a trip to
Los Angeles to audition for
Wheel of Fortune®. Look for
details in all retail Fortune's Children titles!

Look us up on-line at: http://www.romance.net

FC-2-C-R

Take 4 bestselling love stories FREE

Plus get a FREE surprise gift!

Special Limited-time Offer

Mail to Silhouette Reader Service™

3010 Walden Avenue
P.O. Box 1867
Buffalo, N.Y. 14240-1867

YES! Please send me 4 free Silhouette Special Edition® novels and my free surprise gift. Then send me 6 brand-new novels every month, which I will receive months before they appear in bookstores. Bill me at the low price of $3.34 each plus 25¢ delivery and applicable sales tax, if any.* That's the complete price and a savings of over 10% off the cover prices—quite a bargain! I understand that accepting the books and gift places me under no obligation ever to buy any books. I can always return a shipment and cancel at any time. Even if I never buy another book from Silhouette, the 4 free books and the surprise gift are mine to keep forever.

235 BPA A3UV

Name	(PLEASE PRINT)	
Address	Apt. No.	
City	State	Zip

This offer is limited to one order per household and not valid to present Silhouette Special Edition® subscribers. *Terms and prices are subject to change without notice. Sales tax applicable in N.Y.

USPED-696 ©1990 Harlequin Enterprises Limited

You can run, but you cannot hide...from love.

This August, experience danger, excitement and love on the run with three couples thrown together by life-threatening circumstances.

Enjoy three complete stories by some of your favorite authors—all in one special collection!

THE PRINCESS AND THE PEA
by Kathleen Korbel

IN SAFEKEEPING
by Naomi Horton

FUGITIVE
by Emilie Richards

Available this August wherever books are sold.

As seen on TV!
Free Gift Offer

With a Free Gift proof-of-purchase from any Silhouette® book,
you can receive a beautiful cubic zirconia pendant.

This gorgeous marquise-shaped stone is a genuine cubic
zirconia—accented by an 18" gold tone necklace.

(Approximate retail value $19.95)

Send for yours today...
compliments of ▼ *Silhouette*®
™

To receive your free gift, a cubic zirconia pendant, send us one original proof-of-
purchase, photocopies not accepted, from the back of any Silhouette Romance™,
Silhouette Desire®, Silhouette Special Edition®, Silhouette Intimate Moments®
or Silhouette Yours Truly™ title available in August, September or October at your favorite
retail outlet, together with the Free Gift Certificate, plus a check or money order for
$1.65 u.s./$2.15 can. (do not send cash) to cover postage and handling, payable
to Silhouette Free Gift Offer. We will send you the specified gift. Allow 6 to 8 weeks for
delivery. Offer good until October 31, 1996 or while quantities last. Offer valid in the
U.S. and Canada only.

Free Gift Certificate

Name: _____

Address: _____

City: _____ State/Province: _____ Zip/Postal Code: _____

Mail this certificate, one proof-of-purchase and a check or money order for postage
and handling to: SILHOUETTE FREE GIFT OFFER 1996. In the U.S.: 3010 Walden
Avenue, P.O. Box 9077, Buffalo NY 14269-9077. In Canada: P.O. Box 613, Fort Erie,
Ontario L2Z 5X3.

FREE GIFT OFFER   084-KMD
ONE PROOF-OF-PURCHASE
To collect your fabulous FREE GIFT, a cubic zirconia pendant, you must include this
original proof-of-purchase for each gift with the properly completed Free Gift Certificate.

084-KMD

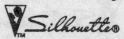

You're About to Become a *Privileged Woman*

Reap the rewards of fabulous free gifts and benefits with proofs-of-purchase from Silhouette and Harlequin books

Pages & Privileges™

It's our way of thanking you for buying our books at your favorite retail stores.

Pages & Privileges™

**Harlequin and Silhouette—
the most privileged readers in the world!**

For more information about Harlequin and Silhouette's PAGES & PRIVILEGES program call the Pages & Privileges Benefits Desk: 1-503-794-2499

Silhouette®

SSE-PP167